THE CREATURE FROM SERENITY SHORE

kaboom!

kaboom! CN CARTOON NETWORK.

BEN 10: THE CREATURE FROM SERENITY SHORE, July 2020. Published by KaBOOM!, a division of Boom Entertainment, Inc.

BOOM! Studios, 5670 Wilshire Boulevard, Suite 400, Los Angeles, CA 90036-5679. Printed in China. First Printing.

ISBN: 978-1-68415-532-3
eISBN: 978-1-64144-698-3

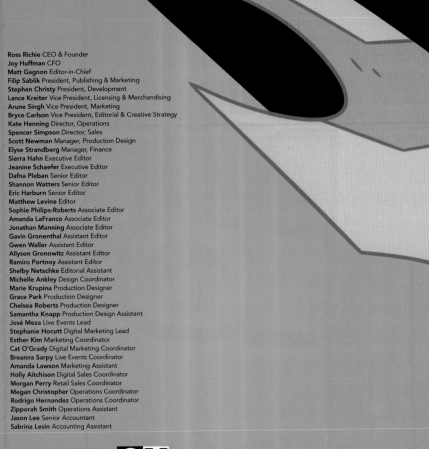

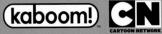

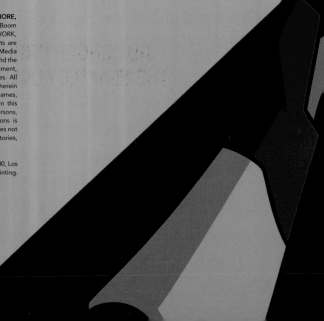

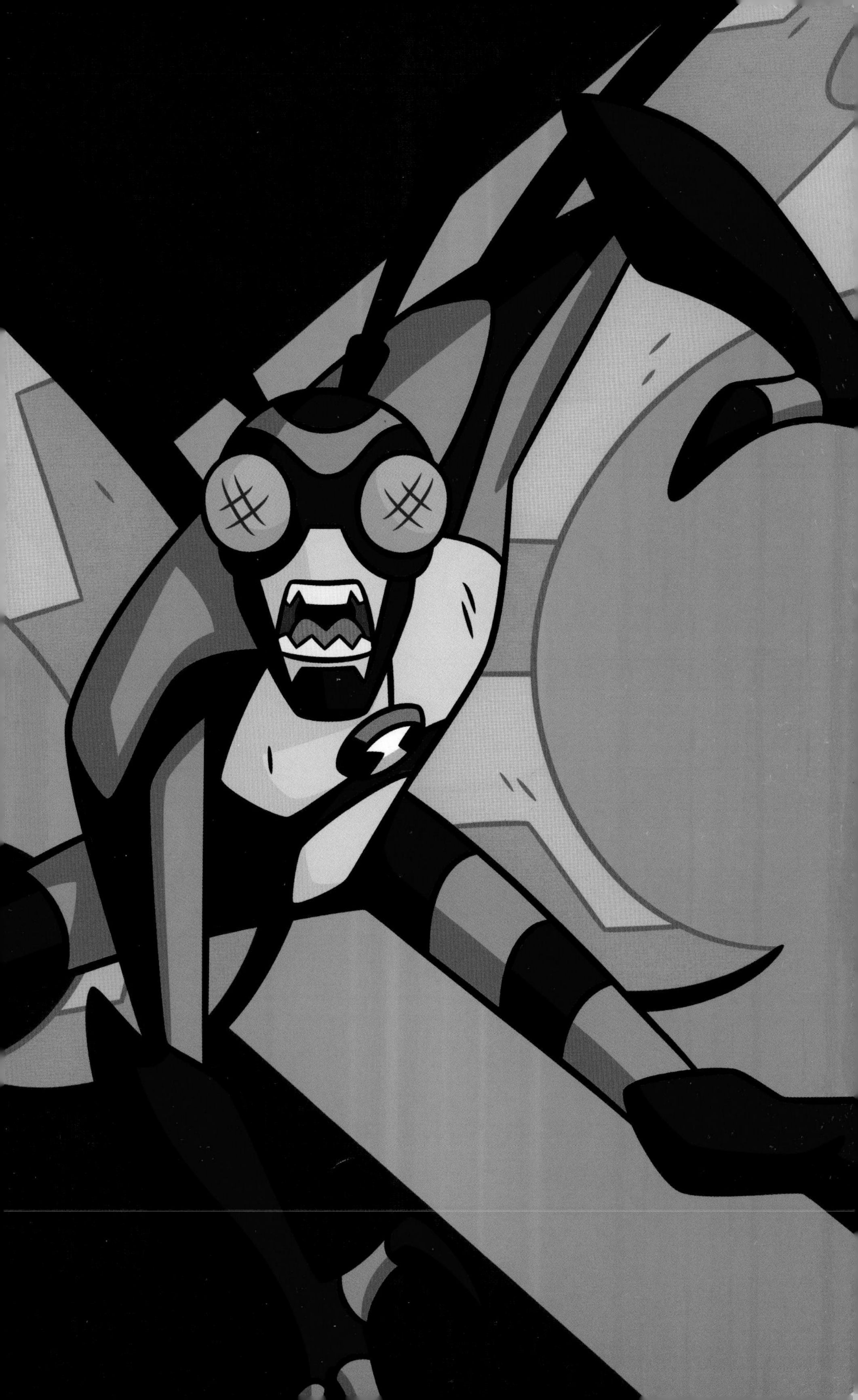

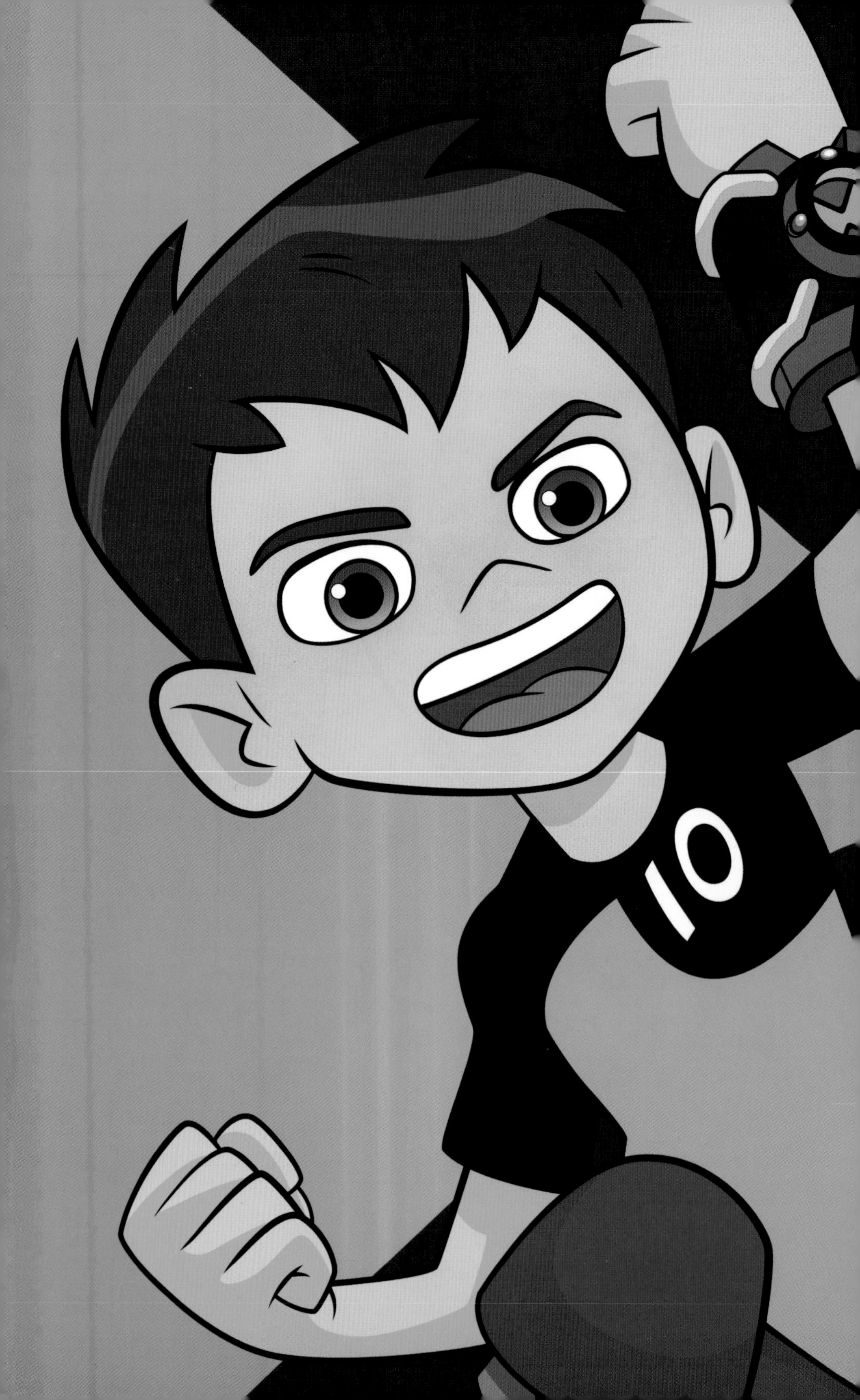
10

BEN TENNYSON IN...

THE CREATURE FROM SERENITY SHORE

CREATED BY
MAN OF ACTION

WRITTEN BY
C.B. LEE

ILLUSTRATED BY
MATTIA DI MEO

COLORED BY
ELEONORA BRUNI

LETTERED BY
WARREN MONTGOMERY

COVER BY
MATTIA DI MEO

DESIGNER
JILLIAN CRAB

EDITOR
MATTHEW LEVINE

WITH SPECIAL THANKS TO
MARISA MARIONAKIS, JANET NO,
AUSTIN PAGE, TRAMM WIGZELL,
KEITH FAY, SHAREENA CARLSON,
AND THE WONDERFUL FOLKS AT
CARTOON NETWORK.

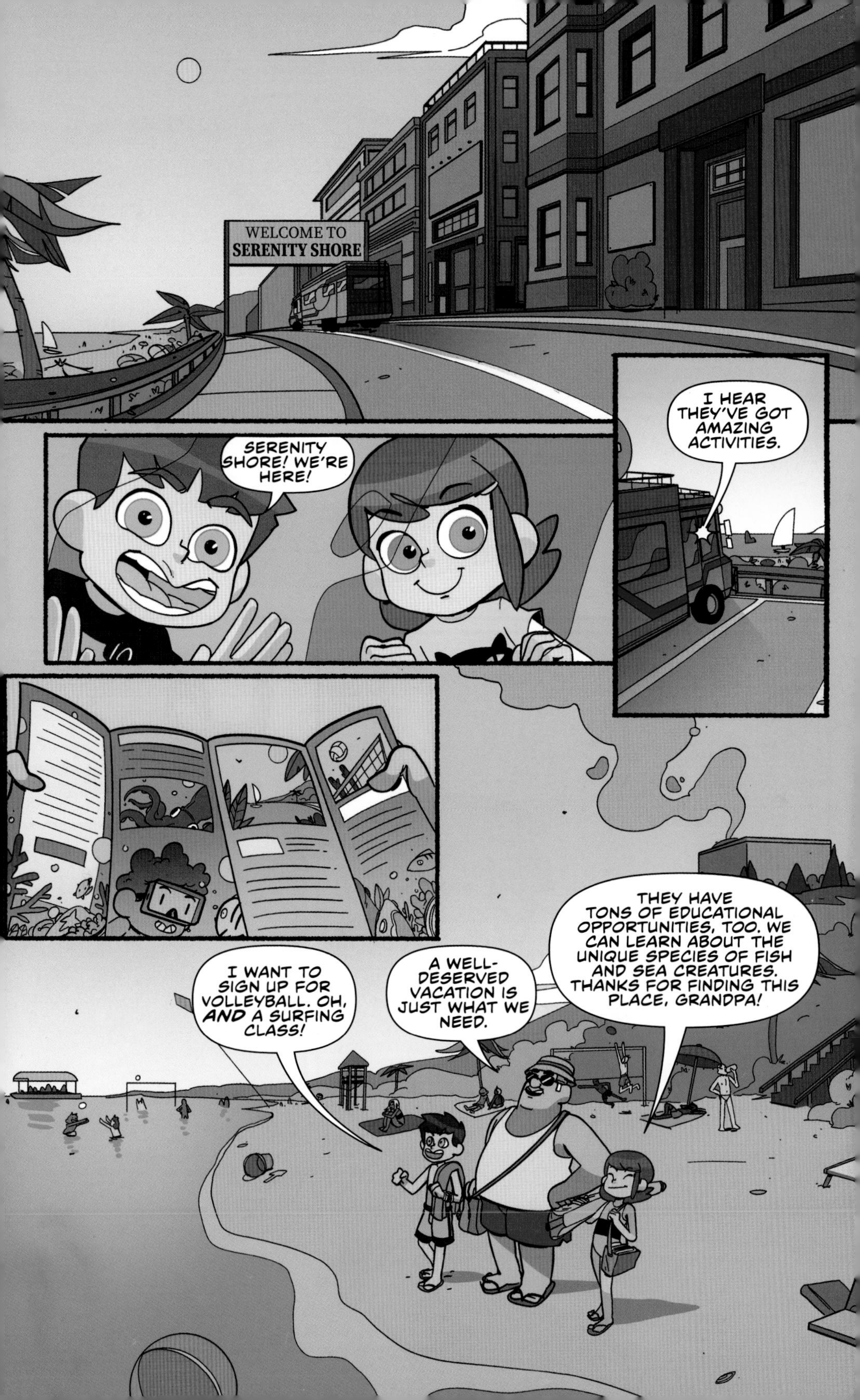
WELCOME TO
SERENITY SHORE
SERENITY SHORE! WE'RE HERE!
I HEAR THEY'VE GOT AMAZING ACTIVITIES.
THEY HAVE TONS OF EDUCATIONAL OPPORTUNITIES, TOO. WE CAN LEARN ABOUT THE UNIQUE SPECIES OF FISH AND SEA CREATURES. THANKS FOR FINDING THIS PLACE, GRANDPA!
I WANT TO SIGN UP FOR VOLLEYBALL. OH, AND A SURFING CLASS!
A WELL-DESERVED VACATION IS JUST WHAT WE NEED.

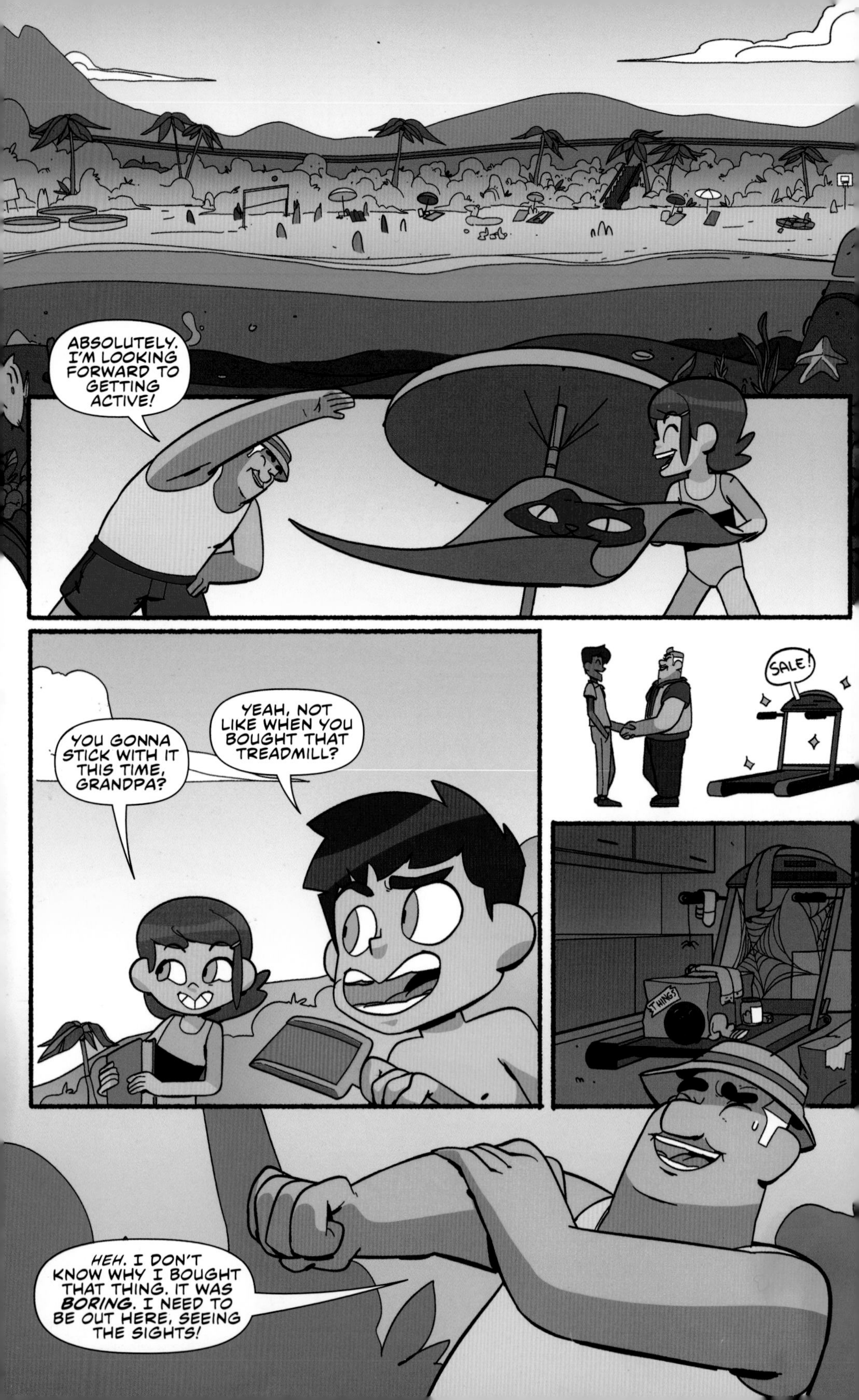
ABSOLUTELY. I'M LOOKING FORWARD TO GETTING ACTIVE!
YOU GONNA STICK WITH IT THIS TIME, GRANDPA?
YEAH, NOT LIKE WHEN YOU BOUGHT THAT TREADMILL?
SALE!
THINGS
HEH. I DON'T KNOW WHY I BOUGHT THAT THING. IT WAS BORING. I NEED TO BE OUT HERE, SEEING THE SIGHTS!

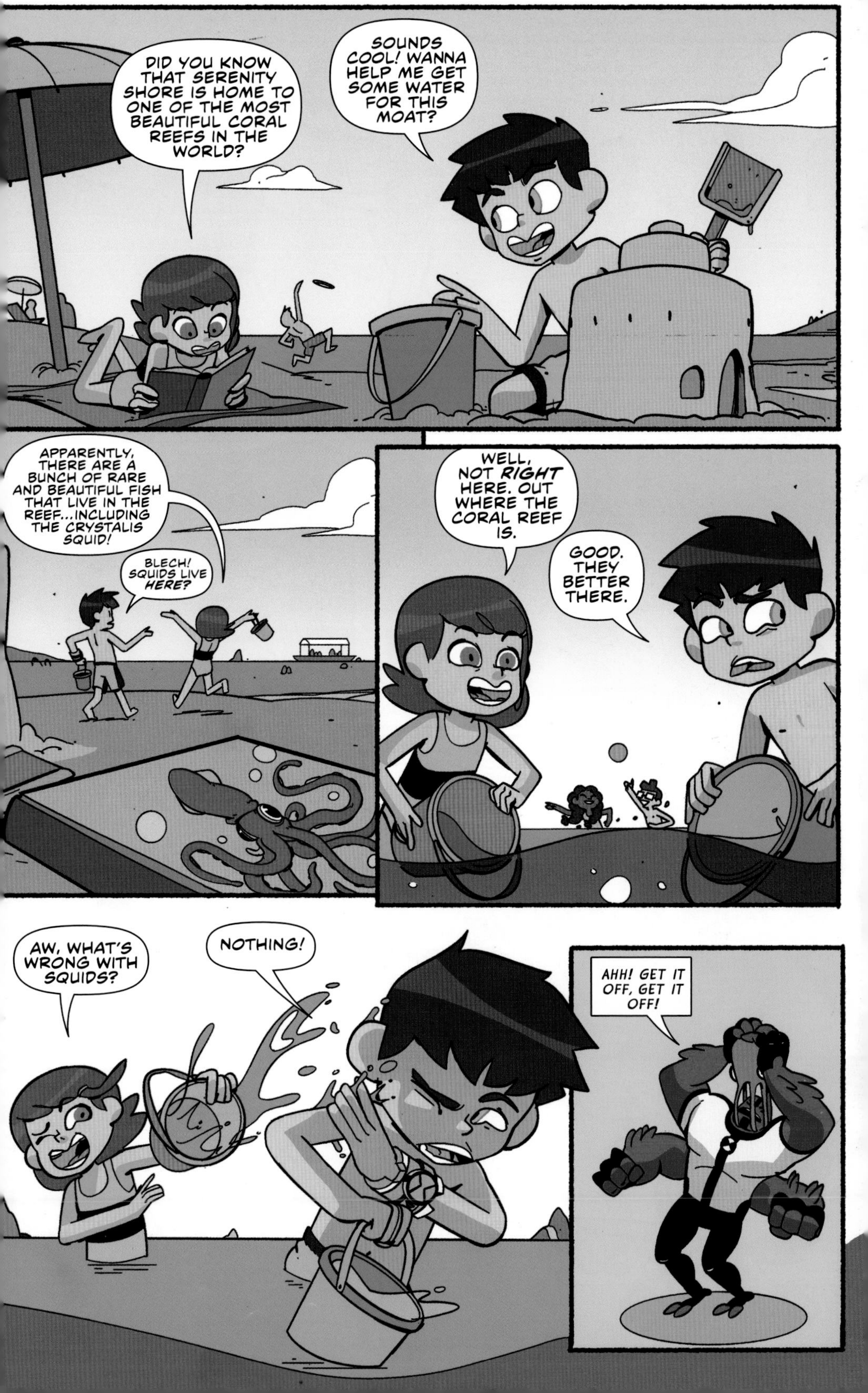
DID YOU KNOW THAT SERENITY SHORE IS HOME TO ONE OF THE MOST BEAUTIFUL CORAL REEFS IN THE WORLD?
SOUNDS COOL! WANNA HELP ME GET SOME WATER FOR THIS MOAT?
APPARENTLY, THERE ARE A BUNCH OF RARE AND BEAUTIFUL FISH THAT LIVE IN THE REEF...INCLUDING THE CRYSTALIS SQUID!
BLECH! SQUIDS LIVE *HERE?*
WELL, NOT *RIGHT* HERE. OUT WHERE THE CORAL REEF IS.
GOOD. THEY BETTER THERE.
AW, WHAT'S WRONG WITH SQUIDS?
NOTHING!
AHH! GET IT OFF, GET IT OFF!

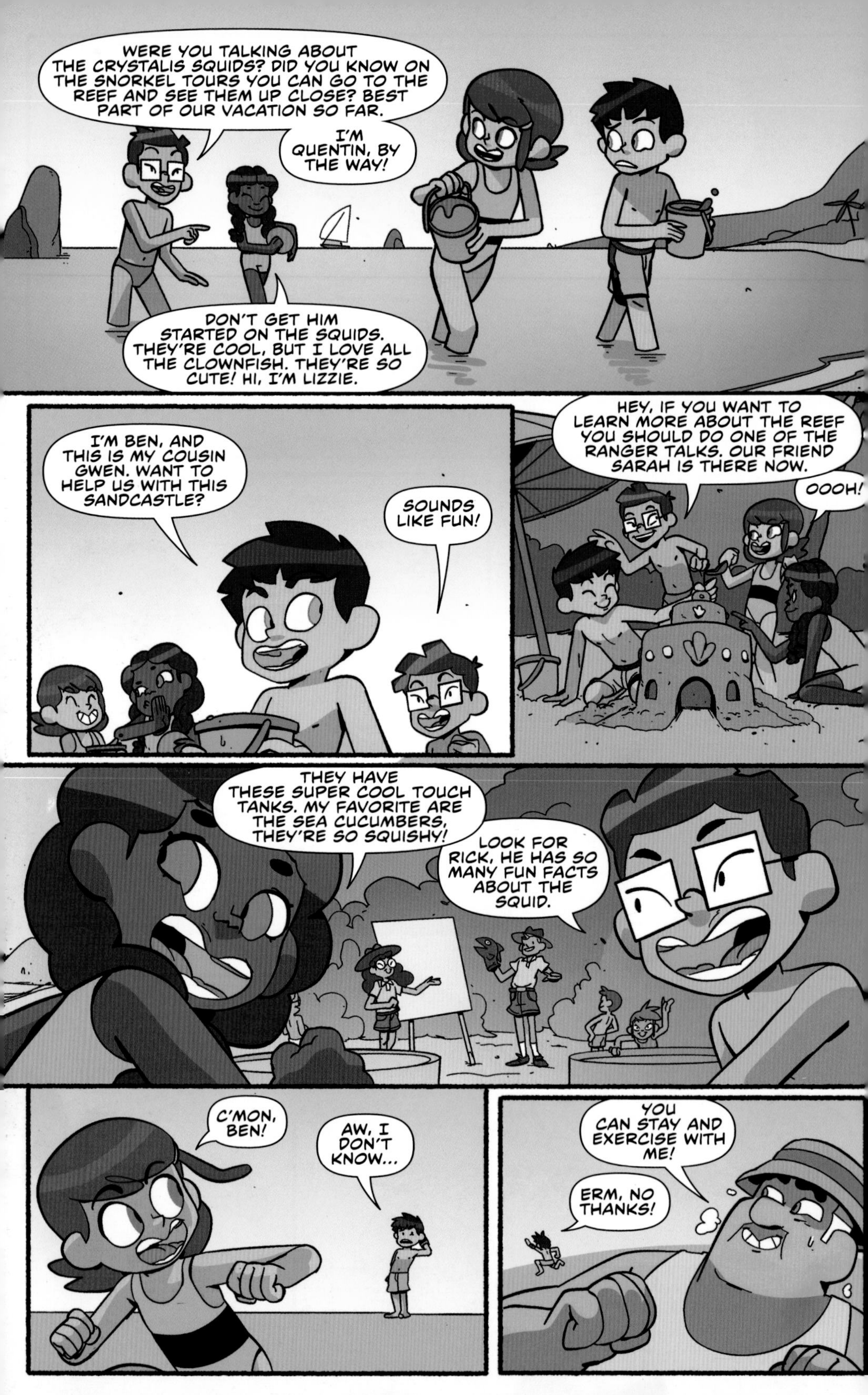
WERE YOU TALKING ABOUT THE CRYSTALIS SQUIDS? DID YOU KNOW ON THE SNORKEL TOURS YOU CAN GO TO THE REEF AND SEE THEM UP CLOSE? BEST PART OF OUR VACATION SO FAR.
I'M QUENTIN, BY THE WAY!
DON'T GET HIM STARTED ON THE SQUIDS. THEY'RE COOL, BUT I LOVE ALL THE CLOWNFISH. THEY'RE SO CUTE! HI, I'M LIZZIE.
I'M BEN, AND THIS IS MY COUSIN GWEN. WANT TO HELP US WITH THIS SANDCASTLE?
SOUNDS LIKE FUN!
HEY, IF YOU WANT TO LEARN MORE ABOUT THE REEF YOU SHOULD DO ONE OF THE RANGER TALKS. OUR FRIEND SARAH IS THERE NOW.
OOOH!
THEY HAVE THESE SUPER COOL TOUCH TANKS. MY FAVORITE ARE THE SEA CUCUMBERS, THEY'RE SO SQUISHY!
LOOK FOR RICK, HE HAS SO MANY FUN FACTS ABOUT THE SQUID.
C'MON, BEN!
AW, I DON'T KNOW...
YOU CAN STAY AND EXERCISE WITH ME!
ERM, NO THANKS!

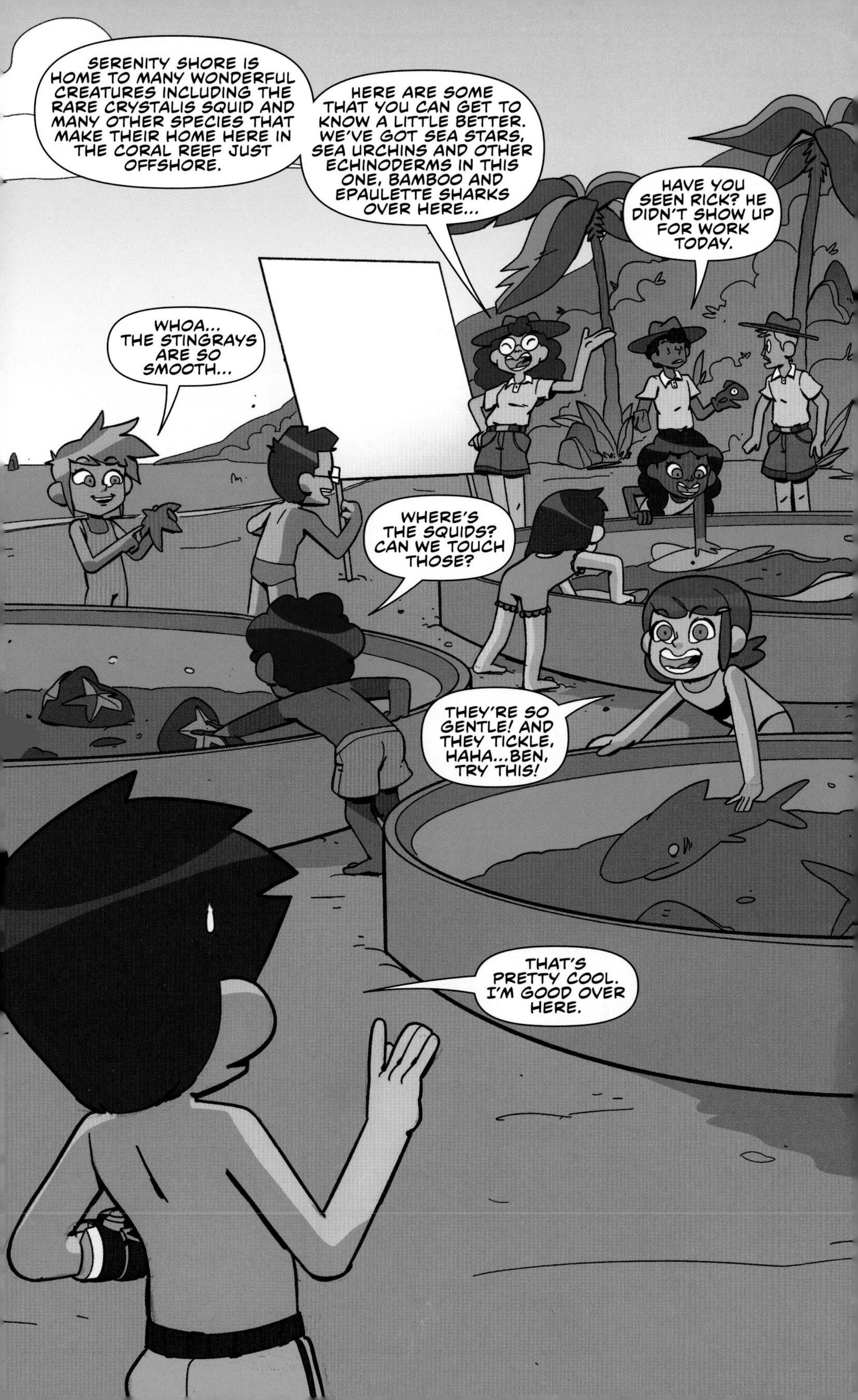
SERENITY SHORE IS HOME TO MANY WONDERFUL CREATURES INCLUDING THE RARE CRYSTALIS SQUID AND MANY OTHER SPECIES THAT MAKE THEIR HOME HERE IN THE CORAL REEF JUST OFFSHORE.
HERE ARE SOME THAT YOU CAN GET TO KNOW A LITTLE BETTER. WE'VE GOT SEA STARS, SEA URCHINS AND OTHER ECHINODERMS IN THIS ONE, BAMBOO AND EPAULETTE SHARKS OVER HERE...
HAVE YOU SEEN RICK? HE DIDN'T SHOW UP FOR WORK TODAY.
WHOA... THE STINGRAYS ARE SO SMOOTH...
WHERE'S THE SQUIDS? CAN WE TOUCH THOSE?
THEY'RE SO GENTLE! AND THEY TICKLE, HAHA...BEN, TRY THIS!
THAT'S PRETTY COOL. I'M GOOD OVER HERE.

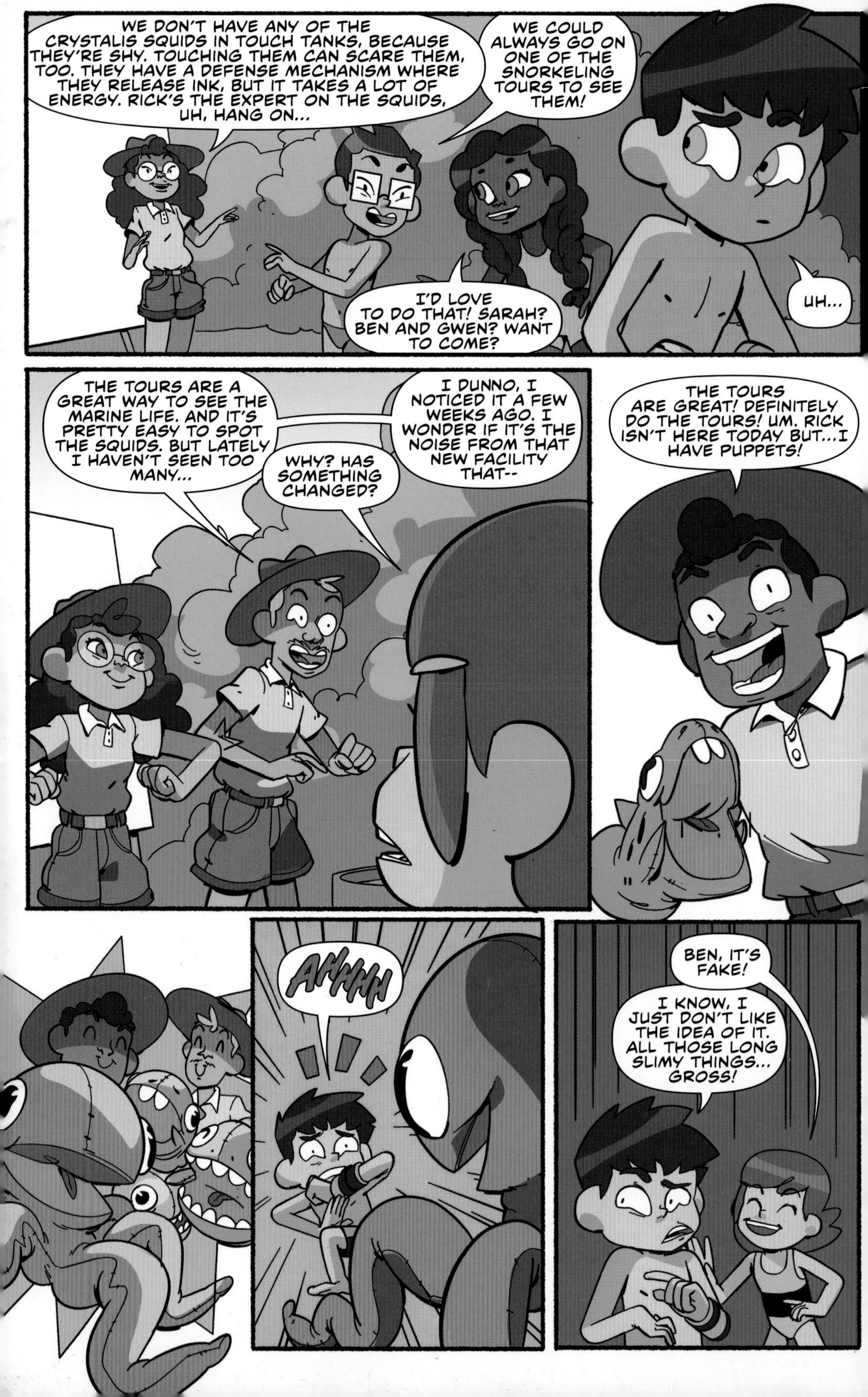
WE DON'T HAVE ANY OF THE CRYSTALIS SQUIDS IN TOUCH TANKS, BECAUSE THEY'RE SHY. TOUCHING THEM CAN SCARE THEM, TOO. THEY HAVE A DEFENSE MECHANISM WHERE THEY RELEASE INK, BUT IT TAKES A LOT OF ENERGY. RICK'S THE EXPERT ON THE SQUIDS, UH, HANG ON...
WE COULD ALWAYS GO ON ONE OF THE SNORKELING TOURS TO SEE THEM!
I'D LOVE TO DO THAT! SARAH? BEN AND GWEN? WANT TO COME?
UH...
THE TOURS ARE A GREAT WAY TO SEE THE MARINE LIFE. AND IT'S PRETTY EASY TO SPOT THE SQUIDS. BUT LATELY I HAVEN'T SEEN TOO MANY...
WHY? HAS SOMETHING CHANGED?
I DUNNO, I NOTICED IT A FEW WEEKS AGO. I WONDER IF IT'S THE NOISE FROM THAT NEW FACILITY THAT--
THE TOURS ARE GREAT! DEFINITELY DO THE TOURS! UM. RICK ISN'T HERE TODAY BUT...I HAVE PUPPETS!
AHHHH
BEN, IT'S FAKE!
I KNOW, I JUST DON'T LIKE THE IDEA OF IT. ALL THOSE LONG SLIMY THINGS... GROSS!

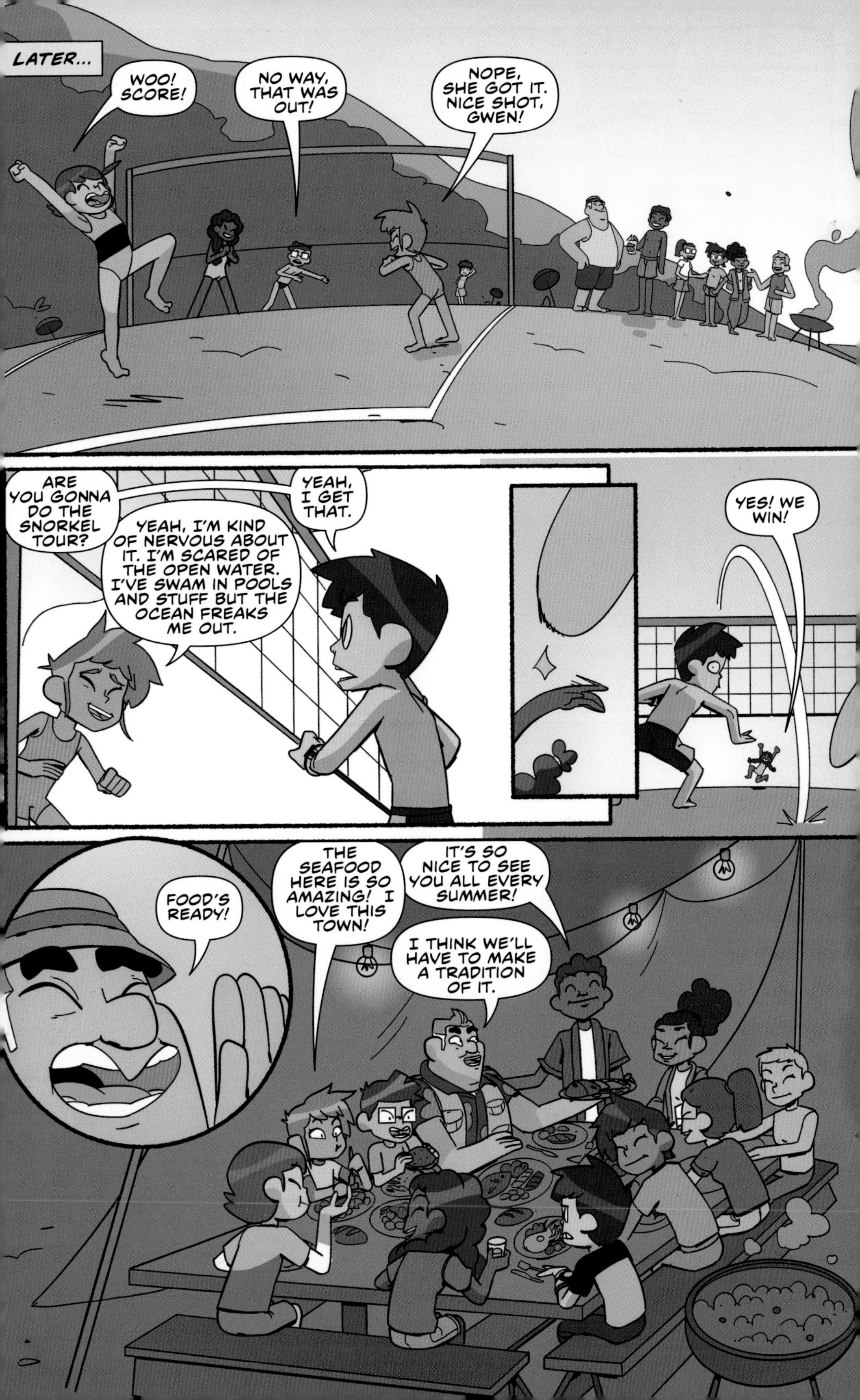
LATER...
WOO! SCORE!
NO WAY, THAT WAS OUT!
NOPE, SHE GOT IT. NICE SHOT, GWEN!
ARE YOU GONNA DO THE SNORKEL TOUR?
YEAH, I'M KIND OF NERVOUS ABOUT IT. I'M SCARED OF THE OPEN WATER. I'VE SWAM IN POOLS AND STUFF BUT THE OCEAN FREAKS ME OUT.
YEAH, I GET THAT.
YES! WE WIN!
FOOD'S READY!
THE SEAFOOD HERE IS SO AMAZING! I LOVE THIS TOWN!
IT'S SO NICE TO SEE YOU ALL EVERY SUMMER!
I THINK WE'LL HAVE TO MAKE A TRADITION OF IT.

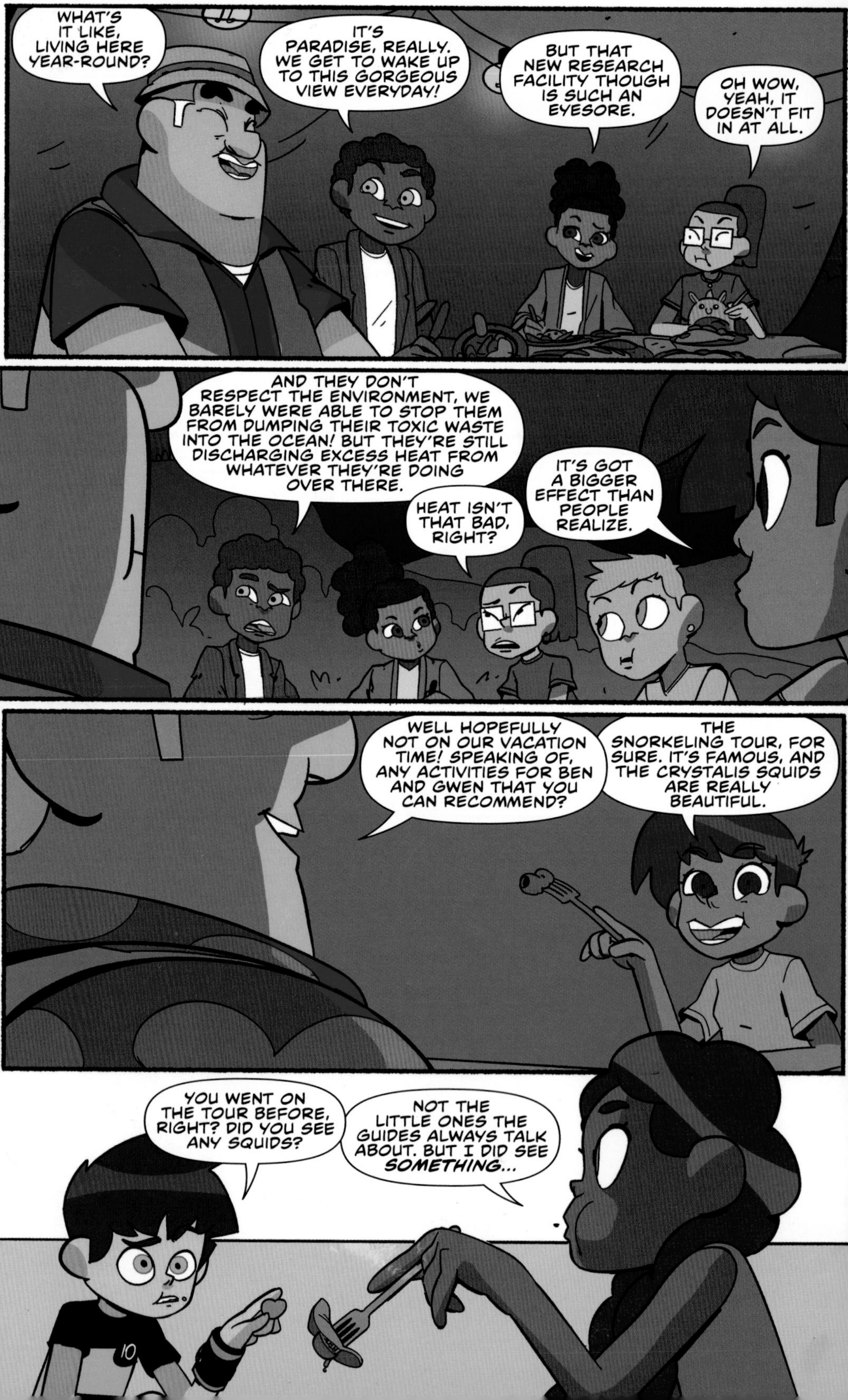
WHAT'S IT LIKE, LIVING HERE YEAR-ROUND?
IT'S PARADISE, REALLY. WE GET TO WAKE UP TO THIS GORGEOUS VIEW EVERYDAY!
BUT THAT NEW RESEARCH FACILITY THOUGH IS SUCH AN EYESORE.
OH WOW, YEAH, IT DOESN'T FIT IN AT ALL.
AND THEY DON'T RESPECT THE ENVIRONMENT, WE BARELY WERE ABLE TO STOP THEM FROM DUMPING THEIR TOXIC WASTE INTO THE OCEAN! BUT THEY'RE STILL DISCHARGING EXCESS HEAT FROM WHATEVER THEY'RE DOING OVER THERE.
HEAT ISN'T THAT BAD, RIGHT?
IT'S GOT A BIGGER EFFECT THAN PEOPLE REALIZE.
WELL HOPEFULLY NOT ON OUR VACATION TIME! SPEAKING OF, ANY ACTIVITIES FOR BEN AND GWEN THAT YOU CAN RECOMMEND?
THE SNORKELING TOUR, FOR SURE. IT'S FAMOUS, AND THE CRYSTALIS SQUIDS ARE REALLY BEAUTIFUL.
YOU WENT ON THE TOUR BEFORE, RIGHT? DID YOU SEE ANY SQUIDS?
NOT THE LITTLE ONES THE GUIDES ALWAYS TALK ABOUT. BUT I DID SEE *SOMETHING*...
10

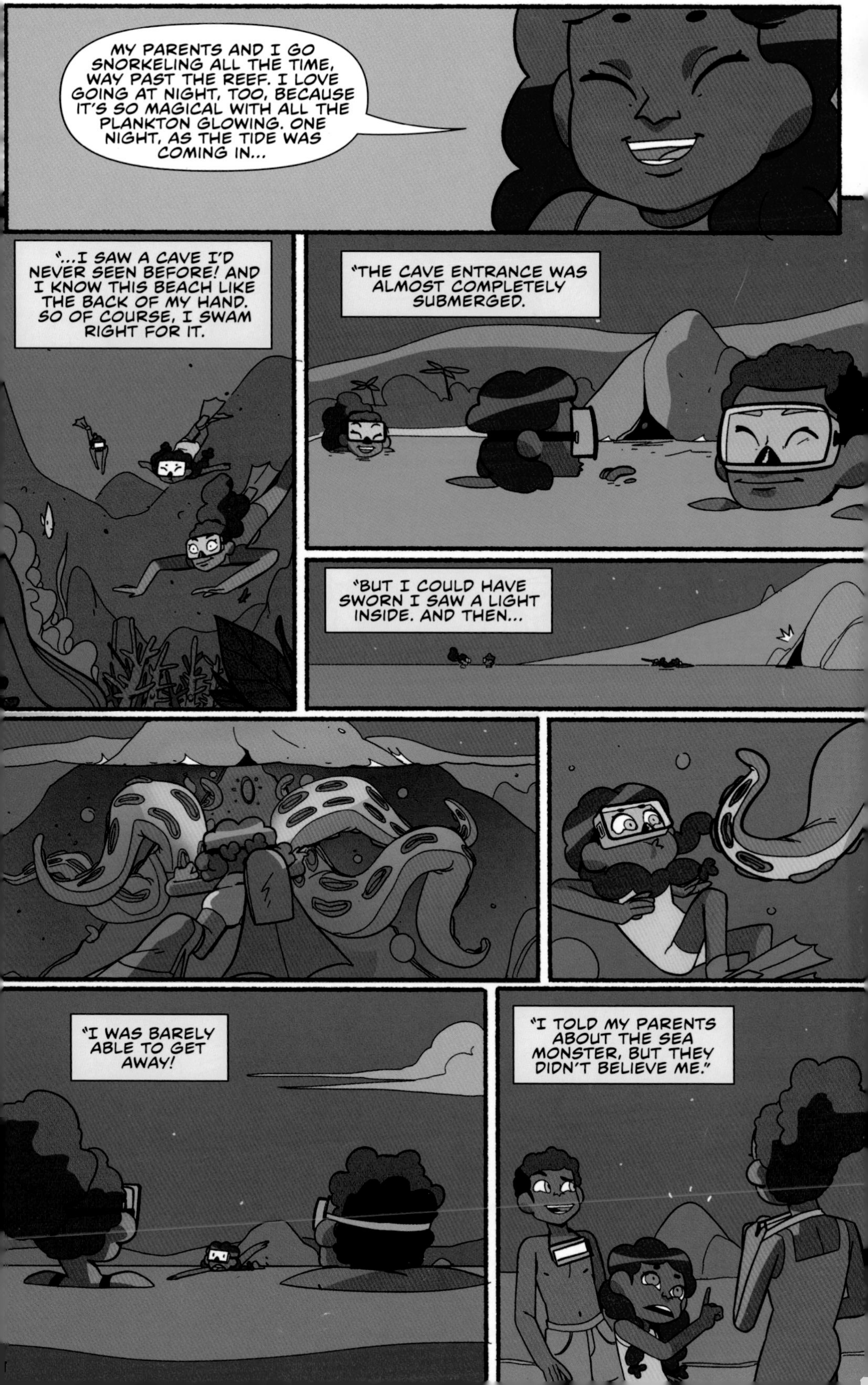
MY PARENTS AND I GO SNORKELING ALL THE TIME, WAY PAST THE REEF. I LOVE GOING AT NIGHT, TOO, BECAUSE IT'S SO MAGICAL WITH ALL THE PLANKTON GLOWING. ONE NIGHT, AS THE TIDE WAS COMING IN...
"...I SAW A CAVE I'D NEVER SEEN BEFORE! AND I KNOW THIS BEACH LIKE THE BACK OF MY HAND. SO OF COURSE, I SWAM RIGHT FOR IT.
"THE CAVE ENTRANCE WAS ALMOST COMPLETELY SUBMERGED.
"BUT I COULD HAVE SWORN I SAW A LIGHT INSIDE. AND THEN...
"I WAS BARELY ABLE TO GET AWAY!
"I TOLD MY PARENTS ABOUT THE SEA MONSTER, BUT THEY DIDN'T BELIEVE ME."

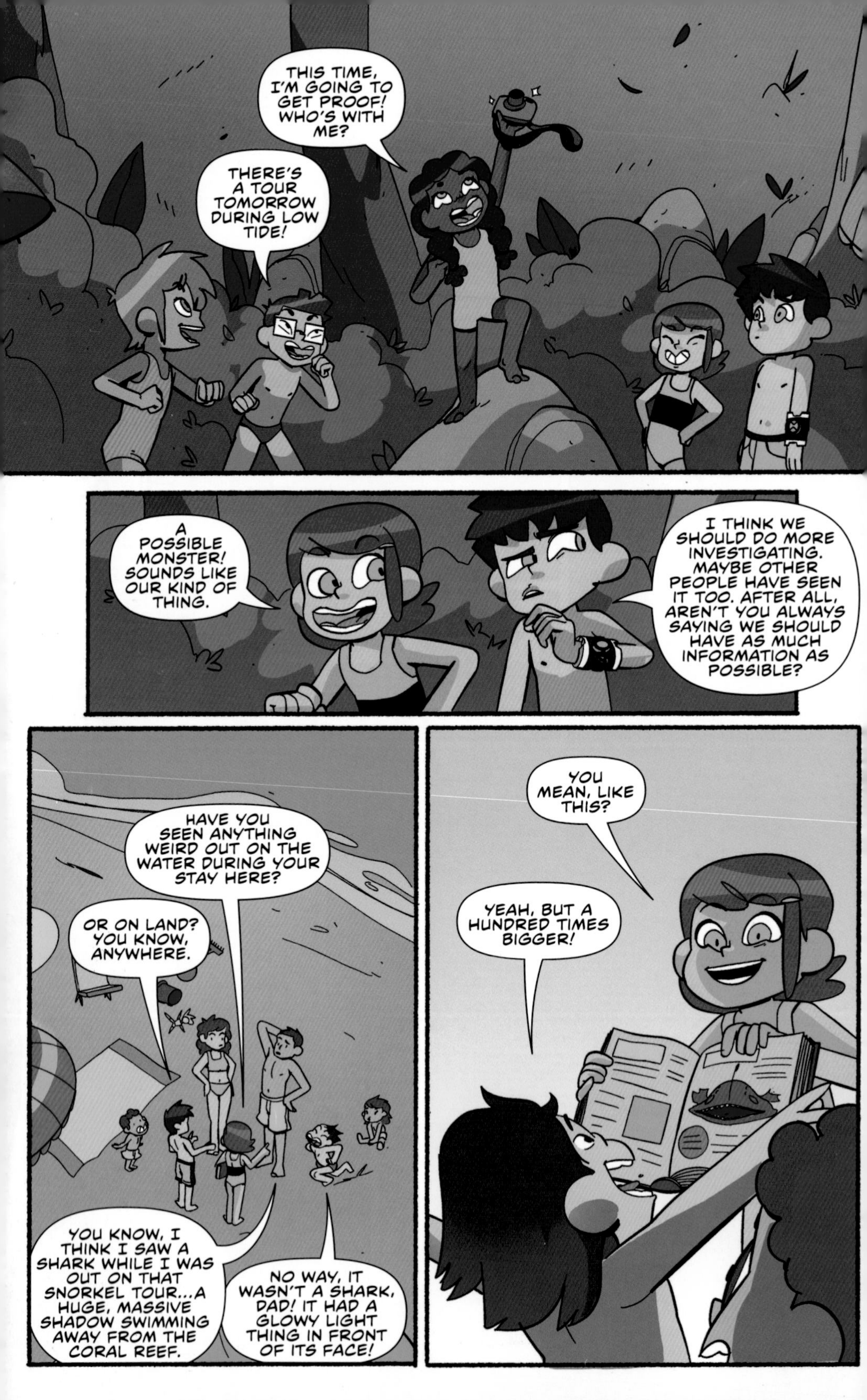

THIS TIME, I'M GOING TO GET PROOF! WHO'S WITH ME?
THERE'S A TOUR TOMORROW DURING LOW TIDE!
A POSSIBLE MONSTER! SOUNDS LIKE OUR KIND OF THING.
I THINK WE SHOULD DO MORE INVESTIGATING. MAYBE OTHER PEOPLE HAVE SEEN IT TOO. AFTER ALL, AREN'T YOU ALWAYS SAYING WE SHOULD HAVE AS MUCH INFORMATION AS POSSIBLE?
HAVE YOU SEEN ANYTHING WEIRD OUT ON THE WATER DURING YOUR STAY HERE?
OR ON LAND? YOU KNOW, ANYWHERE.
YOU KNOW, I THINK I SAW A SHARK WHILE I WAS OUT ON THAT SNORKEL TOUR...A HUGE, MASSIVE SHADOW SWIMMING AWAY FROM THE CORAL REEF.
NO WAY, IT WASN'T A SHARK, DAD! IT HAD A GLOWY LIGHT THING IN FRONT OF ITS FACE!
YOU MEAN, LIKE THIS?
YEAH, BUT A HUNDRED TIMES BIGGER!

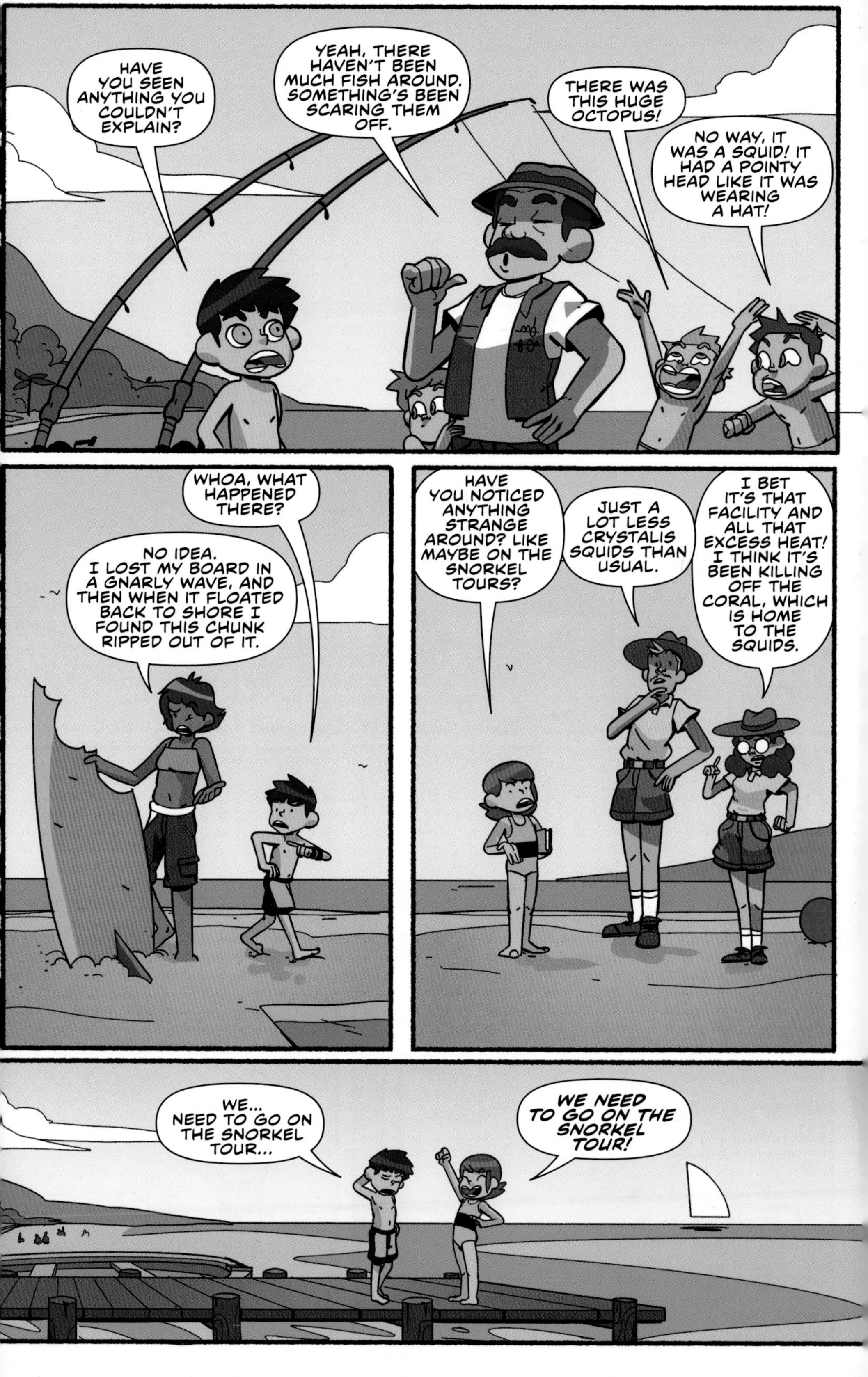
HAVE YOU SEEN ANYTHING YOU COULDN'T EXPLAIN?
YEAH, THERE HAVEN'T BEEN MUCH FISH AROUND. SOMETHING'S BEEN SCARING THEM OFF.
THERE WAS THIS HUGE OCTOPUS!
NO WAY, IT WAS A SQUID! IT HAD A POINTY HEAD LIKE IT WAS WEARING A HAT!
WHOA, WHAT HAPPENED THERE?
NO IDEA. I LOST MY BOARD IN A GNARLY WAVE, AND THEN WHEN IT FLOATED BACK TO SHORE I FOUND THIS CHUNK RIPPED OUT OF IT.
HAVE YOU NOTICED ANYTHING STRANGE AROUND? LIKE MAYBE ON THE SNORKEL TOURS?
JUST A LOT LESS CRYSTALIS SQUIDS THAN USUAL.
I BET IT'S THAT FACILITY AND ALL THAT EXCESS HEAT! I THINK IT'S BEEN KILLING OFF THE CORAL, WHICH IS HOME TO THE SQUIDS.
WE... NEED TO GO ON THE SNORKEL TOUR...
WE NEED TO GO ON THE SNORKEL TOUR!

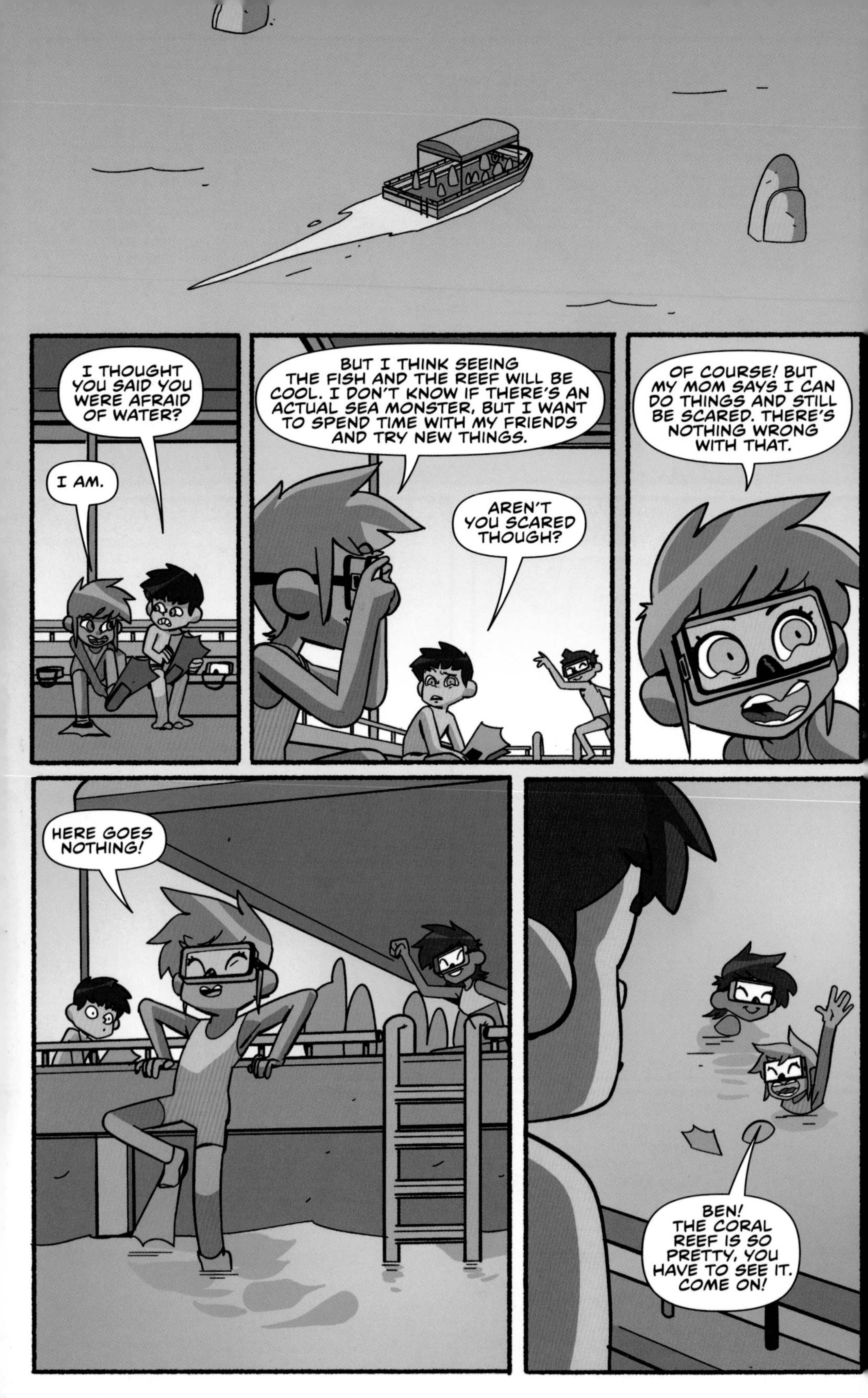
I THOUGHT YOU SAID YOU WERE AFRAID OF WATER?
I AM.
BUT I THINK SEEING THE FISH AND THE REEF WILL BE COOL. I DON'T KNOW IF THERE'S AN ACTUAL SEA MONSTER, BUT I WANT TO SPEND TIME WITH MY FRIENDS AND TRY NEW THINGS.
AREN'T YOU SCARED THOUGH?
OF COURSE! BUT MY MOM SAYS I CAN DO THINGS AND STILL BE SCARED. THERE'S NOTHING WRONG WITH THAT.
HERE GOES NOTHING!
BEN! THE CORAL REEF IS SO PRETTY, YOU HAVE TO SEE IT. COME ON!

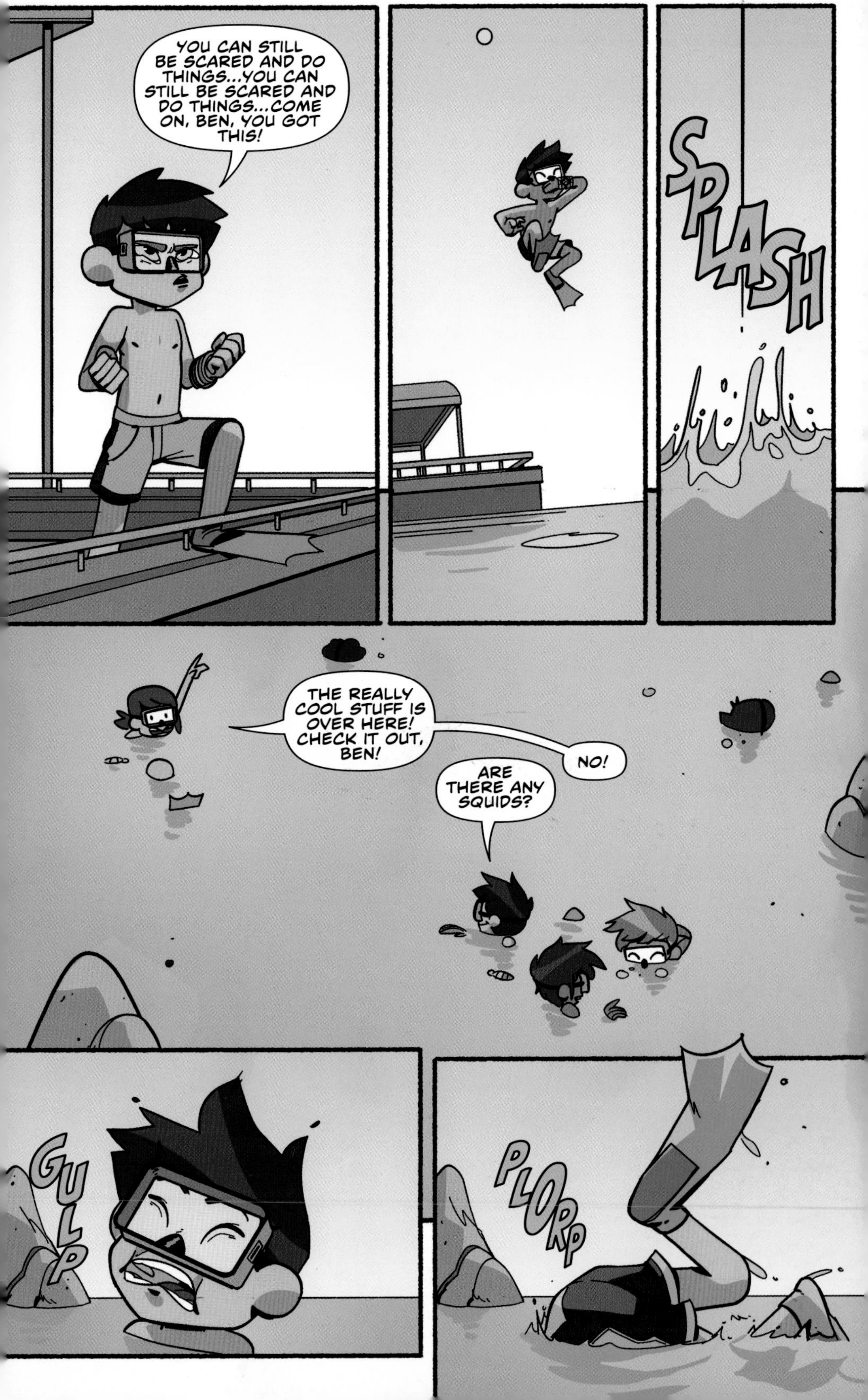
YOU CAN STILL BE SCARED AND DO THINGS...YOU CAN STILL BE SCARED AND DO THINGS...COME ON, BEN, YOU GOT THIS!
SPLASH
THE REALLY COOL STUFF IS OVER HERE! CHECK IT OUT, BEN!
NO!
ARE THERE ANY SQUIDS?
GULP
PLORP

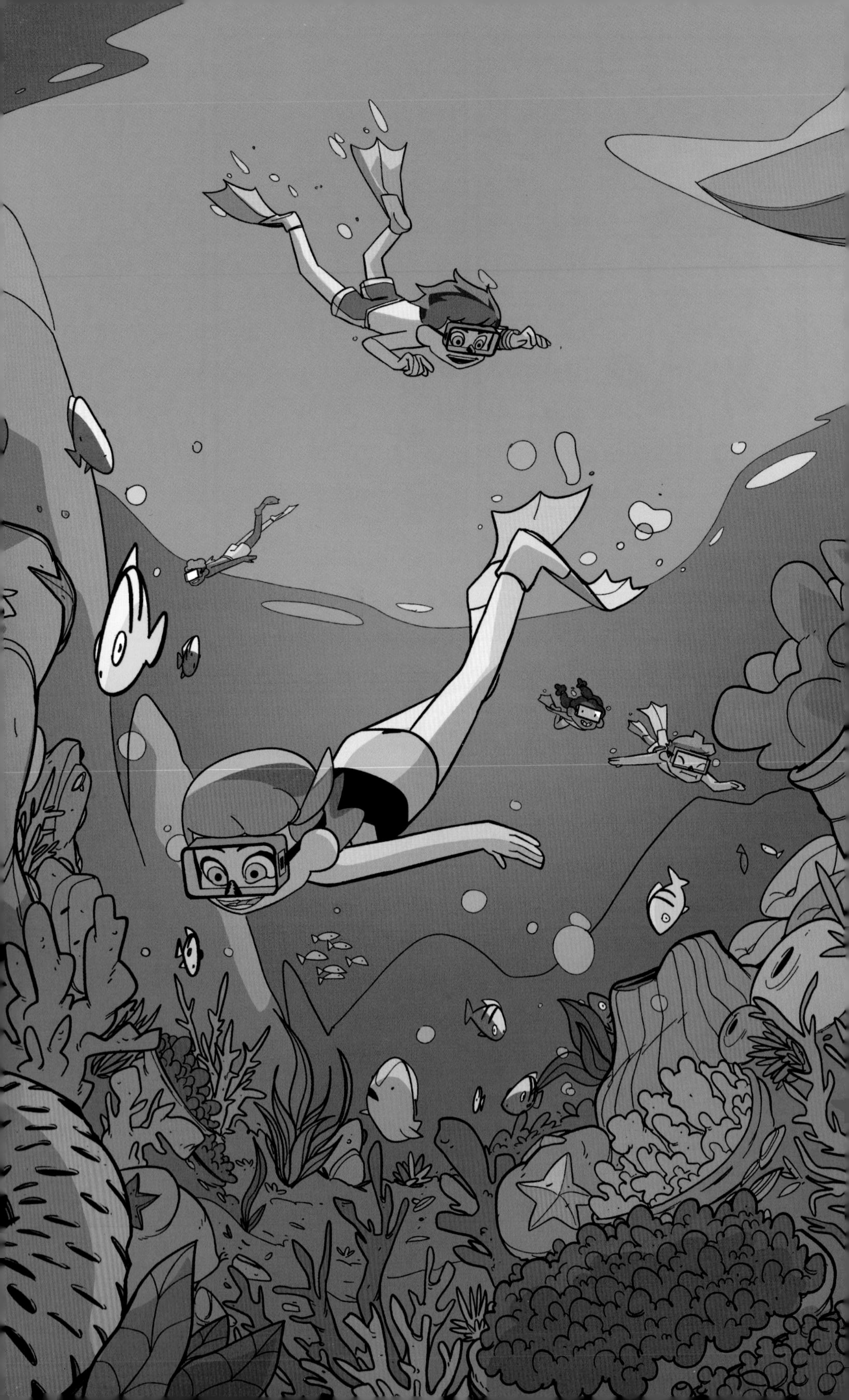

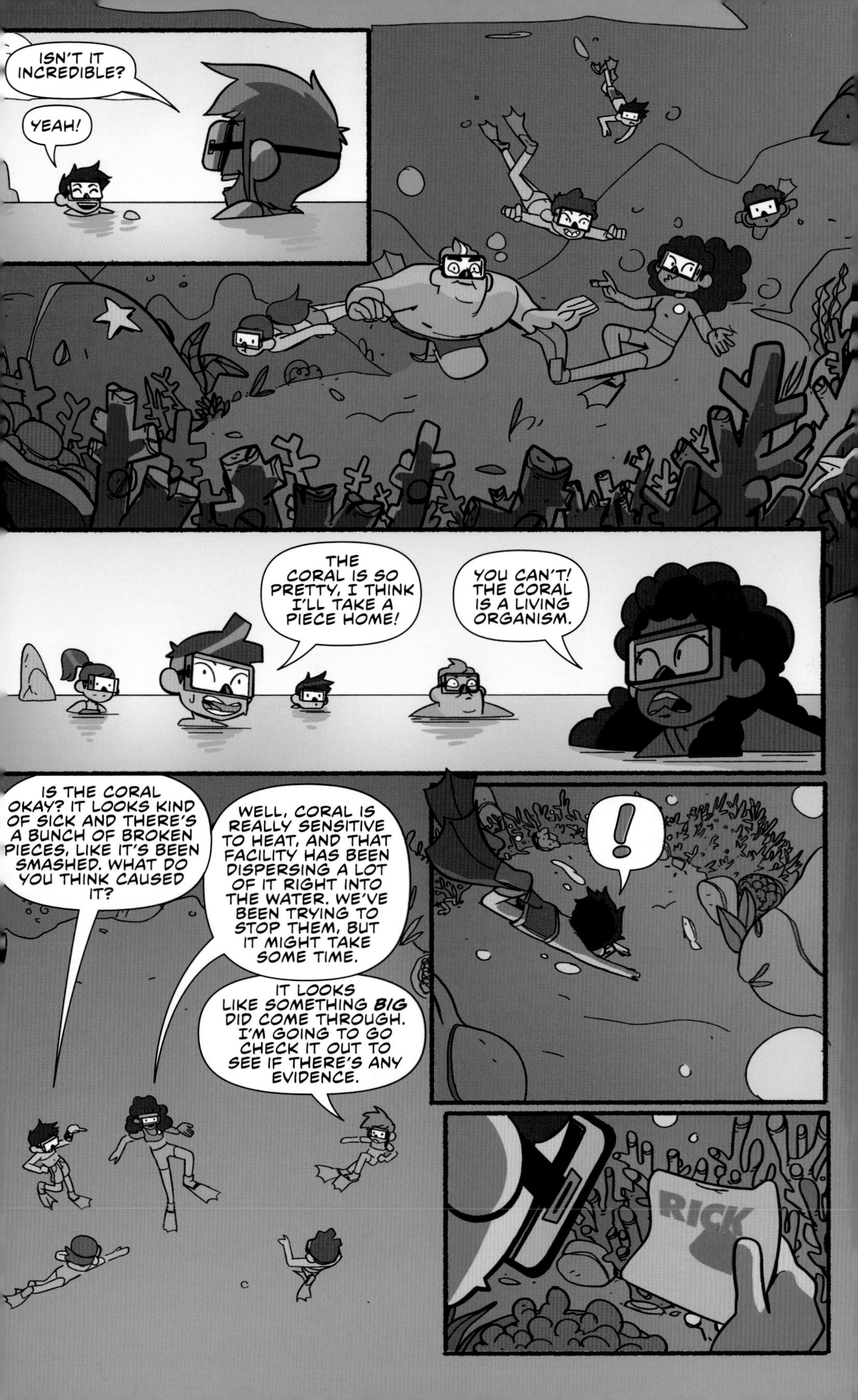
ISN'T IT INCREDIBLE?
YEAH!
THE CORAL IS SO PRETTY, I THINK I'LL TAKE A PIECE HOME!
YOU CAN'T! THE CORAL IS A LIVING ORGANISM.
IS THE CORAL OKAY? IT LOOKS KIND OF SICK AND THERE'S A BUNCH OF BROKEN PIECES, LIKE IT'S BEEN SMASHED. WHAT DO YOU THINK CAUSED IT?
WELL, CORAL IS REALLY SENSITIVE TO HEAT, AND THAT FACILITY HAS BEEN DISPERSING A LOT OF IT RIGHT INTO THE WATER. WE'VE BEEN TRYING TO STOP THEM, BUT IT MIGHT TAKE SOME TIME.
IT LOOKS LIKE SOMETHING *BIG* DID COME THROUGH. I'M GOING TO GO CHECK IT OUT TO SEE IF THERE'S ANY EVIDENCE.
!
RICK

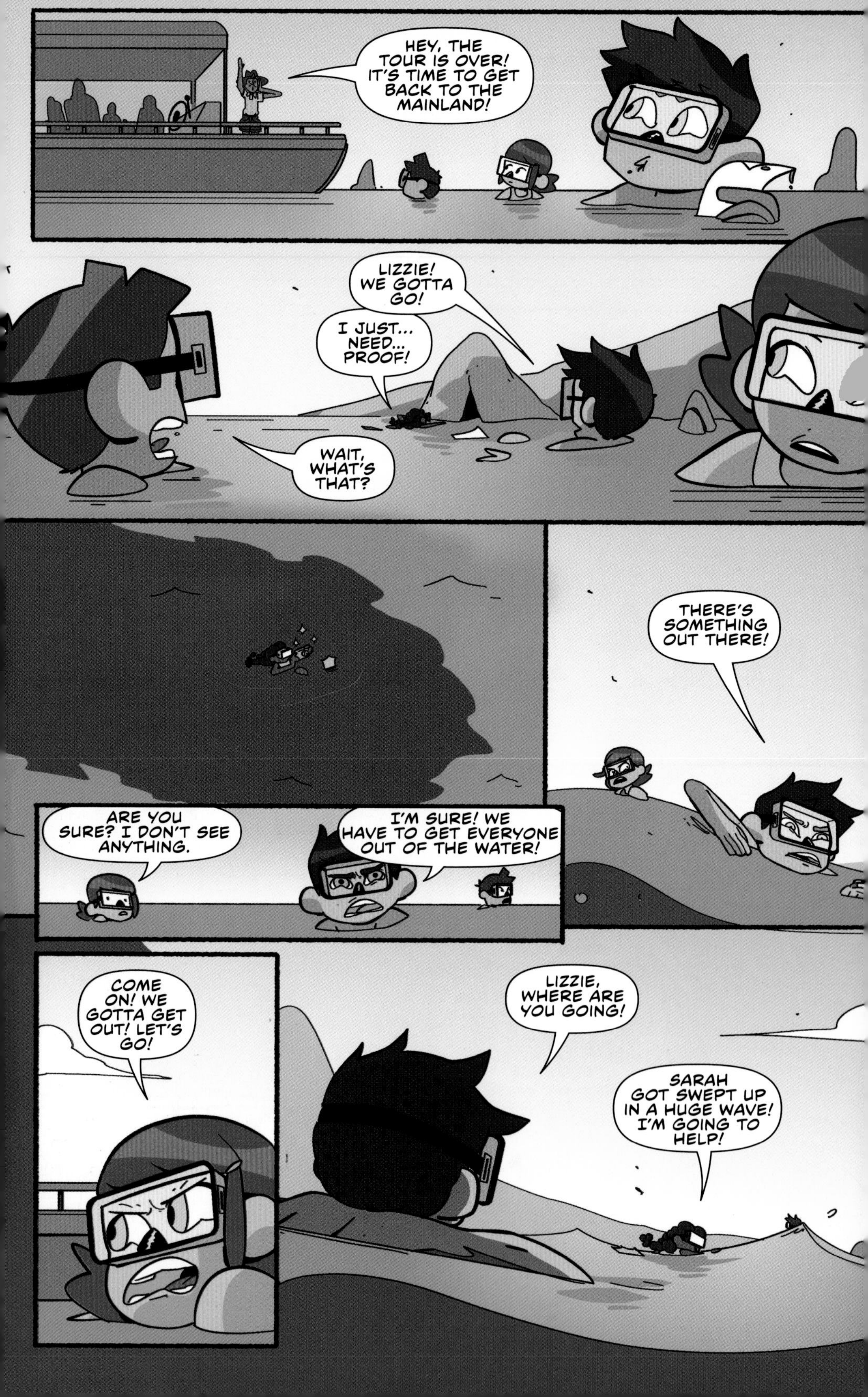
HEY, THE TOUR IS OVER! IT'S TIME TO GET BACK TO THE MAINLAND!
LIZZIE! WE GOTTA GO!
I JUST... NEED... PROOF!
WAIT, WHAT'S THAT?
THERE'S SOMETHING OUT THERE!
ARE YOU SURE? I DON'T SEE ANYTHING.
I'M SURE! WE HAVE TO GET EVERYONE OUT OF THE WATER!
COME ON! WE GOTTA GET OUT! LET'S GO!
LIZZIE, WHERE ARE YOU GOING!
SARAH GOT SWEPT UP IN A HUGE WAVE! I'M GOING TO HELP!

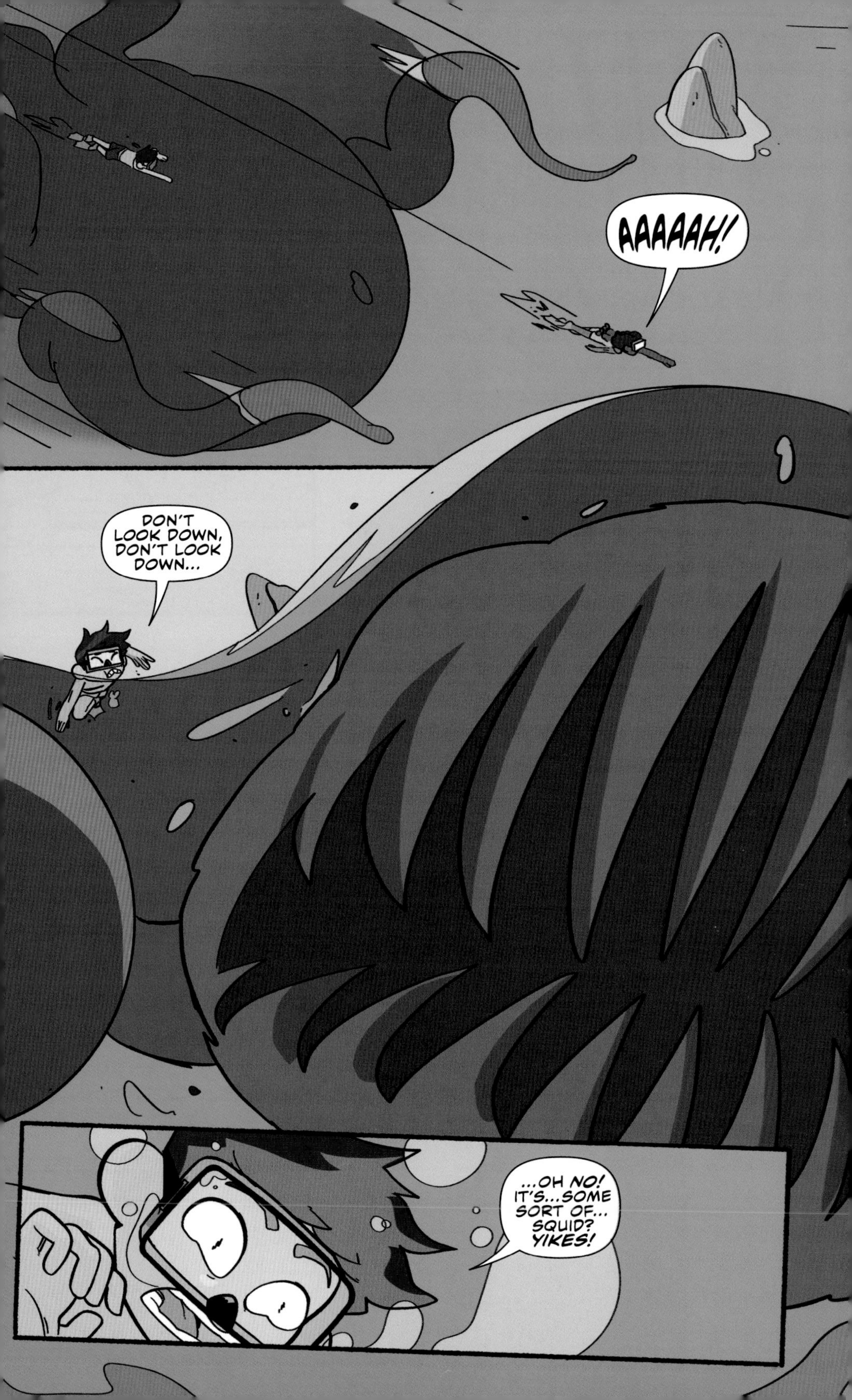
AAAAAH!
DON'T LOOK DOWN, DON'T LOOK DOWN...
...OH NO! IT'S...SOME SORT OF... SQUID? YIKES!

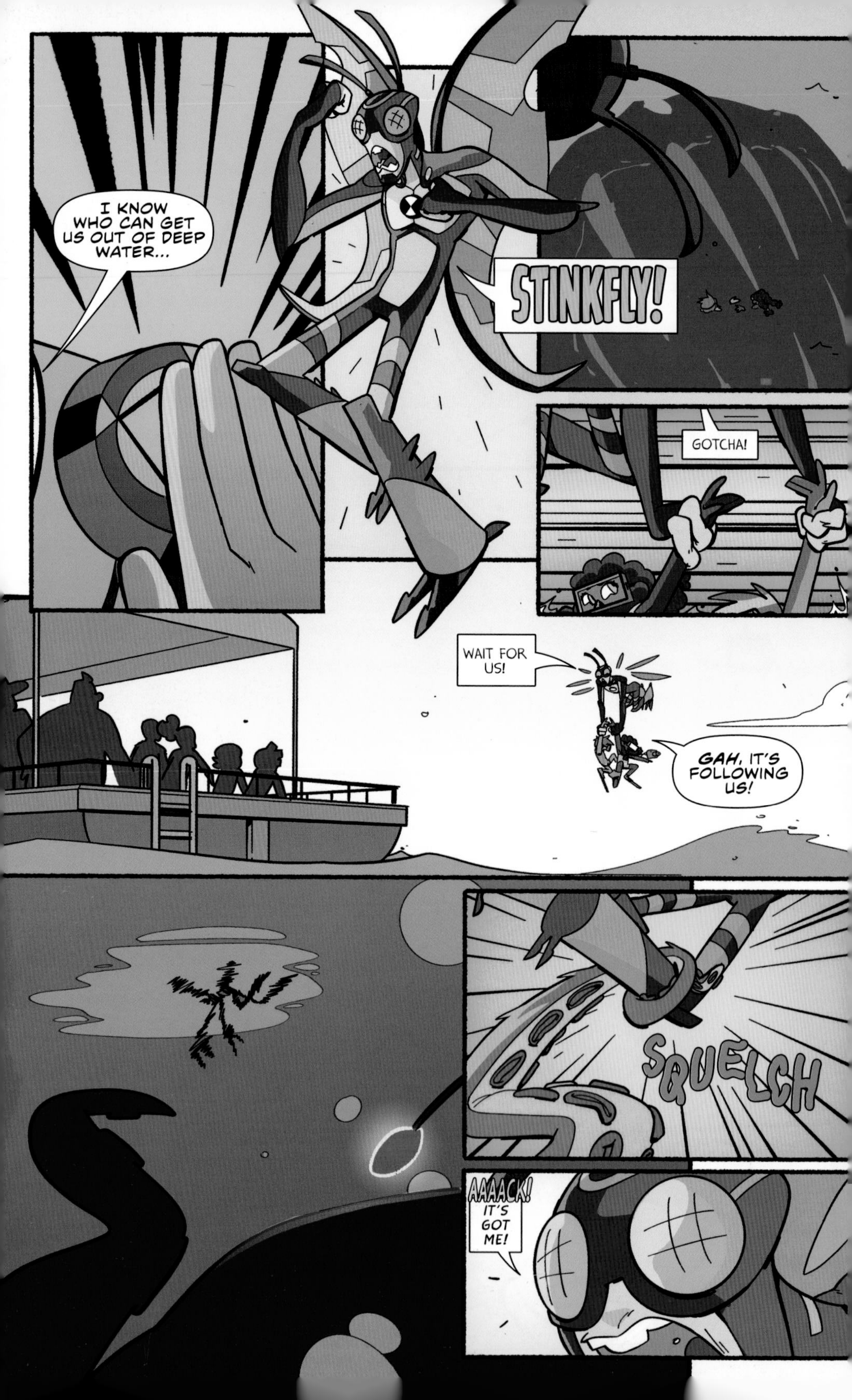
I KNOW WHO CAN GET US OUT OF DEEP WATER...
STINKFLY!
GOTCHA!
WAIT FOR US!
GAH, IT'S FOLLOWING US!
SQUELCH
AAAACK! IT'S GOT ME!

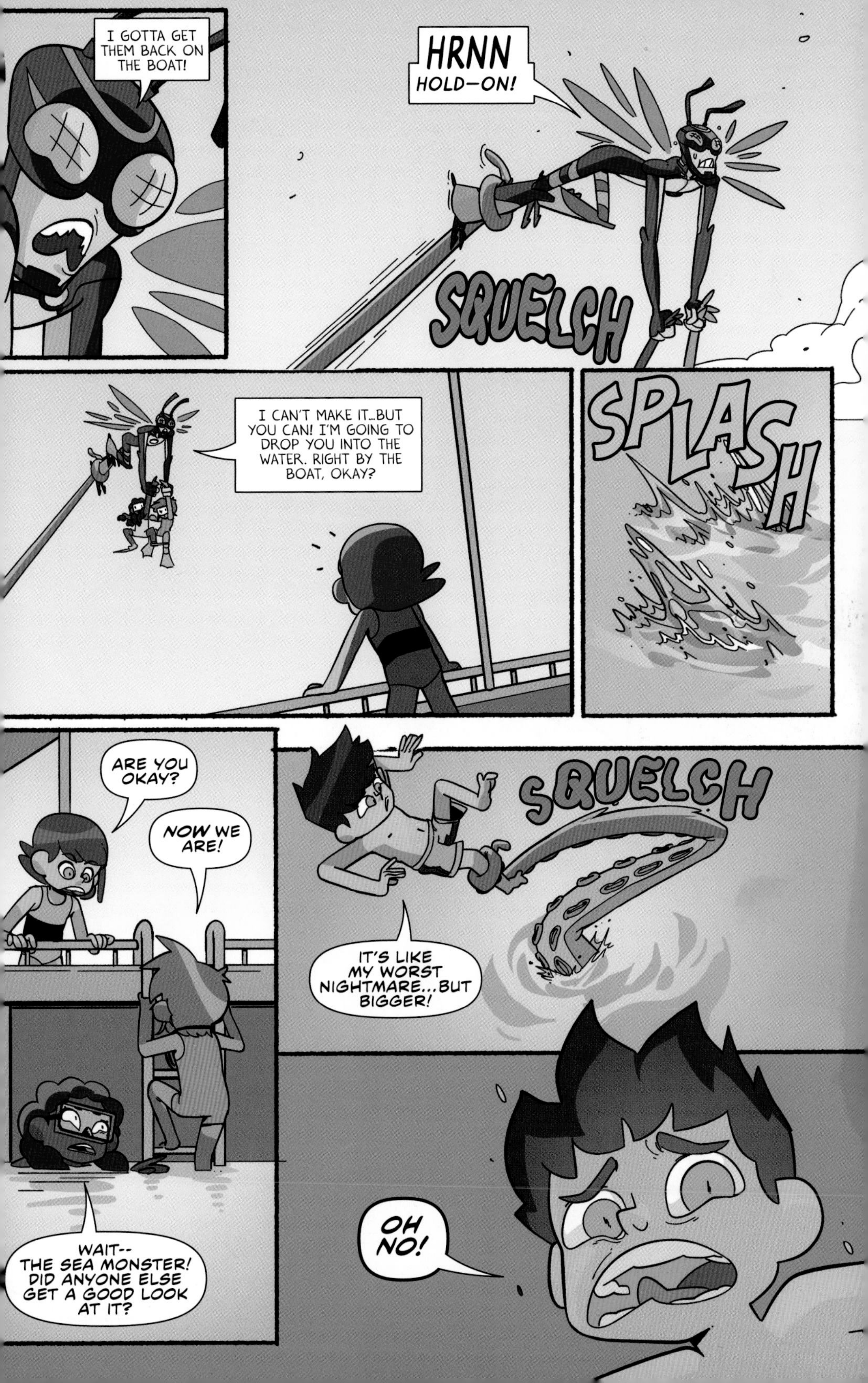
I GOTTA GET THEM BACK ON THE BOAT!
HRNN
HOLD—ON!
SQUELCH
I CAN'T MAKE IT...BUT YOU CAN! I'M GOING TO DROP YOU INTO THE WATER. RIGHT BY THE BOAT, OKAY?
SPLASH
ARE YOU OKAY?
NOW WE ARE!
WAIT-- THE SEA MONSTER! DID ANYONE ELSE GET A GOOD LOOK AT IT?
SQUELCH
IT'S LIKE MY WORST NIGHTMARE...BUT BIGGER!
OH NO!

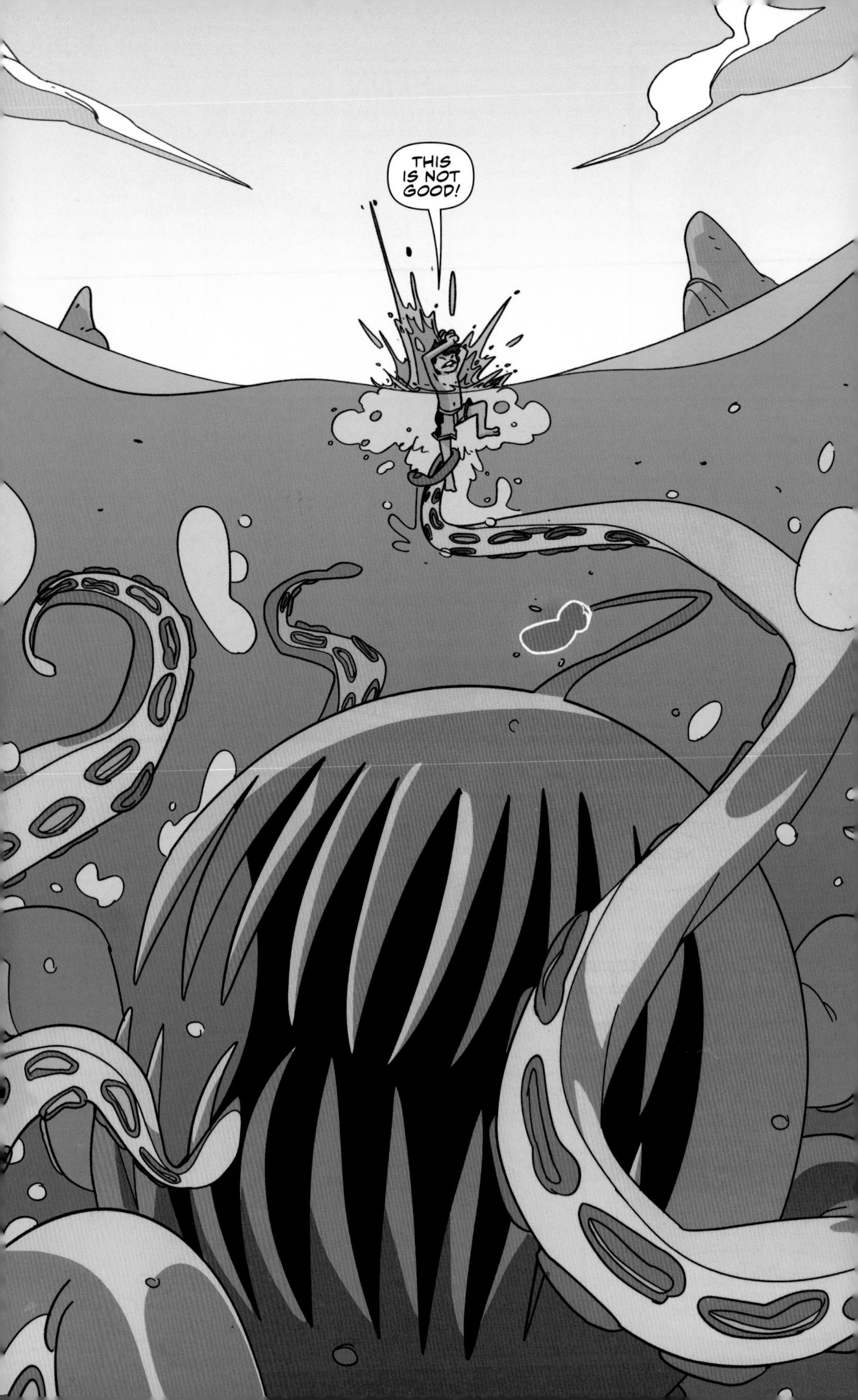
THIS IS NOT GOOD!

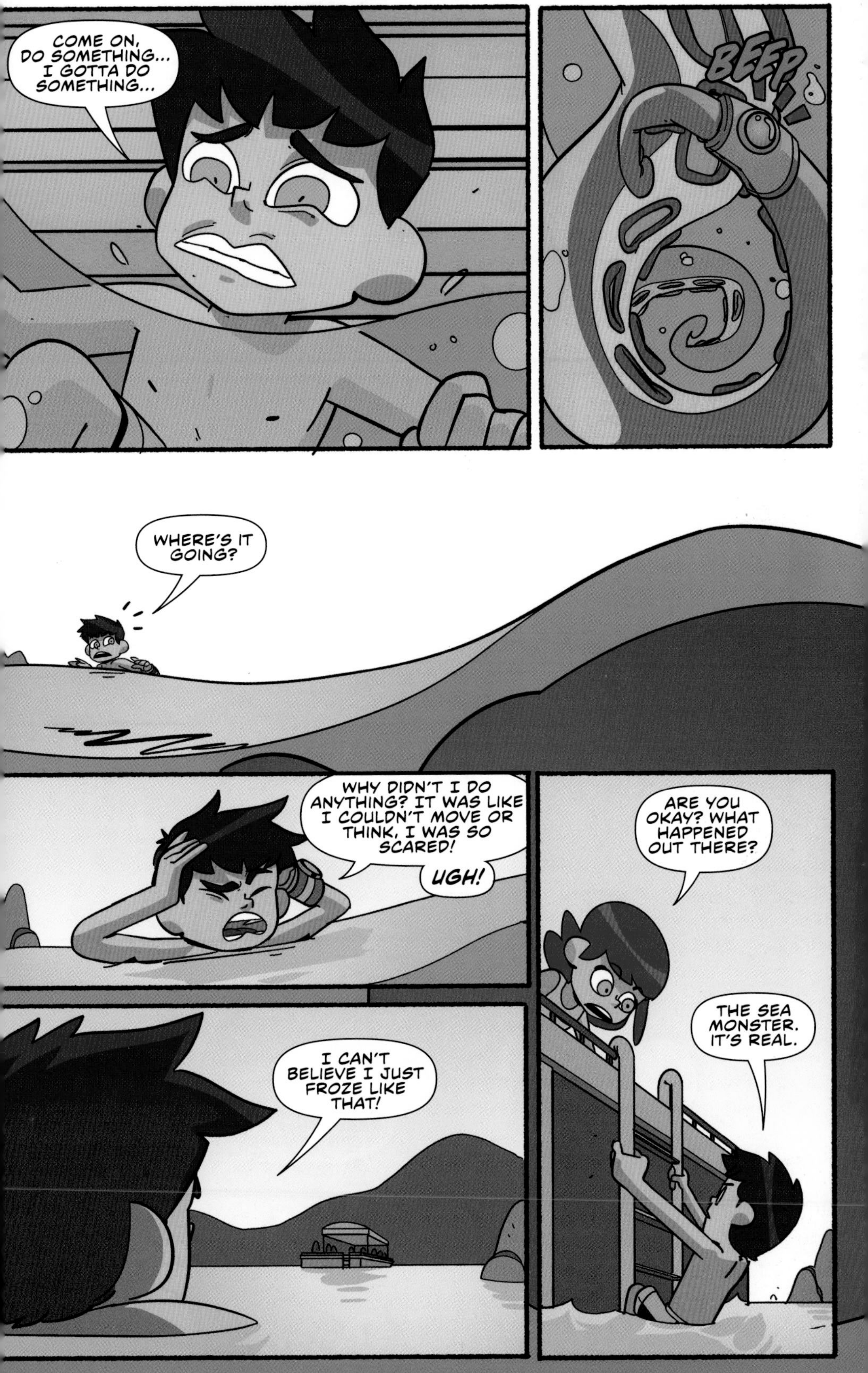
COME ON, DO SOMETHING... I GOTTA DO SOMETHING...
BEEP
WHERE'S IT GOING?
WHY DIDN'T I DO ANYTHING? IT WAS LIKE I COULDN'T MOVE OR THINK, I WAS SO SCARED!
UGH!
I CAN'T BELIEVE I JUST FROZE LIKE THAT!
ARE YOU OKAY? WHAT HAPPENED OUT THERE?
THE SEA MONSTER. IT'S REAL.

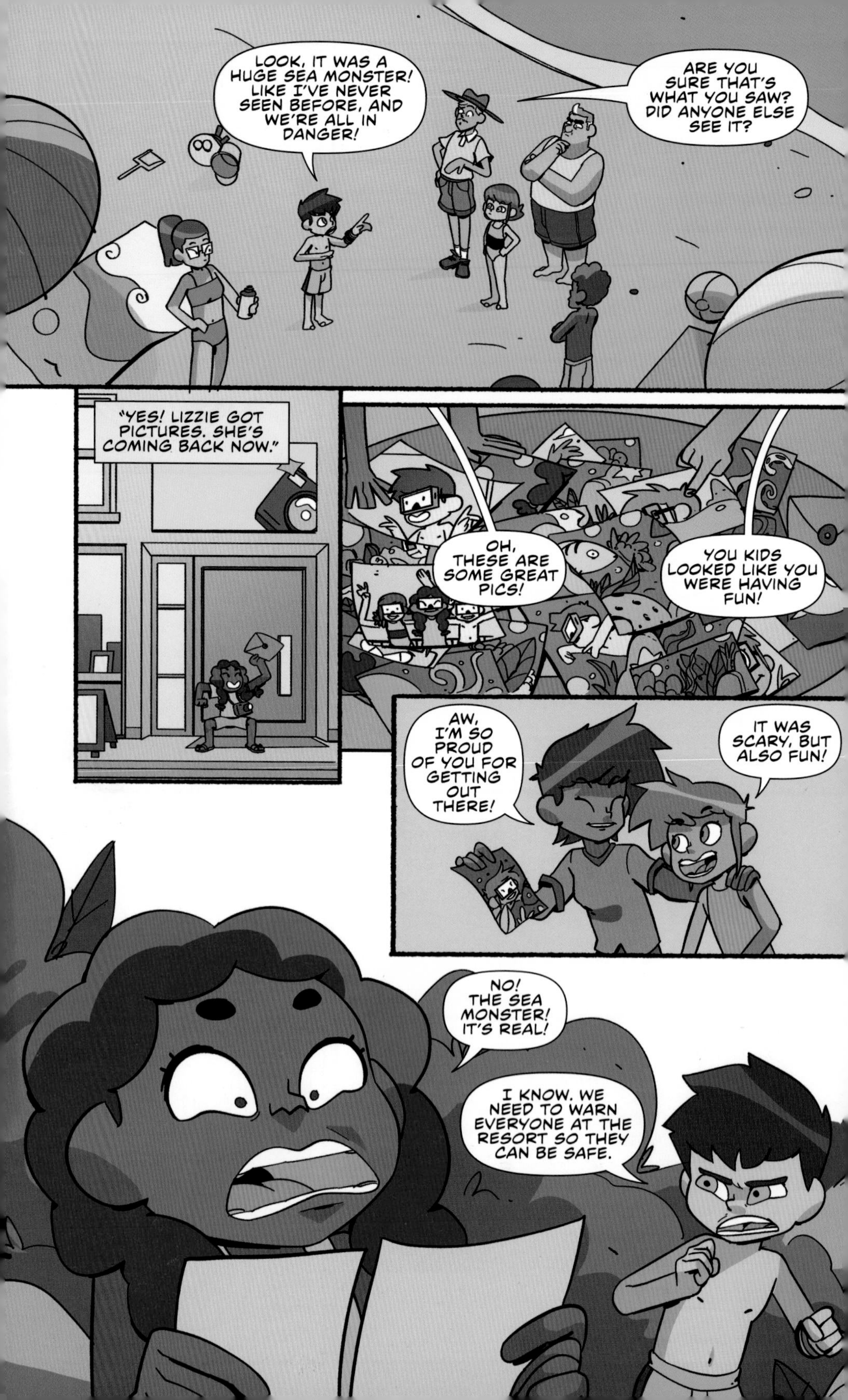
LOOK, IT WAS A HUGE SEA MONSTER! LIKE I'VE NEVER SEEN BEFORE, AND WE'RE ALL IN DANGER!
ARE YOU SURE THAT'S WHAT YOU SAW? DID ANYONE ELSE SEE IT?
"YES! LIZZIE GOT PICTURES. SHE'S COMING BACK NOW."
OH, THESE ARE SOME GREAT PICS!
YOU KIDS LOOKED LIKE YOU WERE HAVING FUN!
AW, I'M SO PROUD OF YOU FOR GETTING OUT THERE!
IT WAS SCARY, BUT ALSO FUN!
NO! THE SEA MONSTER! IT'S REAL!
I KNOW. WE NEED TO WARN EVERYONE AT THE RESORT SO THEY CAN BE SAFE.

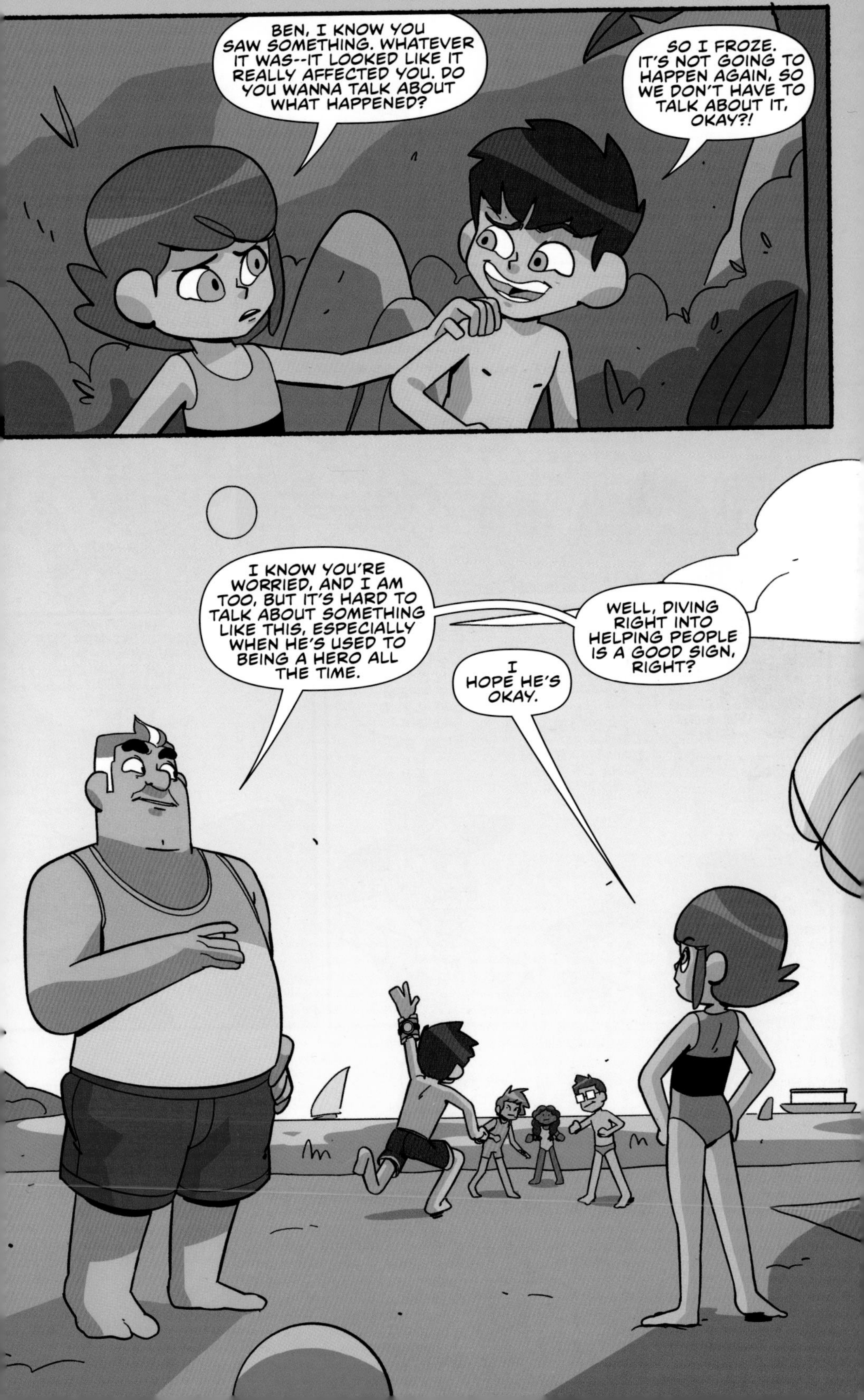
BEN, I KNOW YOU SAW SOMETHING. WHATEVER IT WAS--IT LOOKED LIKE IT REALLY AFFECTED YOU. DO YOU WANNA TALK ABOUT WHAT HAPPENED?
SO I FROZE. IT'S NOT GOING TO HAPPEN AGAIN, SO WE DON'T HAVE TO TALK ABOUT IT, OKAY?!
I HOPE HE'S OKAY.
I KNOW YOU'RE WORRIED, AND I AM TOO, BUT IT'S HARD TO TALK ABOUT SOMETHING LIKE THIS, ESPECIALLY WHEN HE'S USED TO BEING A HERO ALL THE TIME.
WELL, DIVING RIGHT INTO HELPING PEOPLE IS A GOOD SIGN, RIGHT?

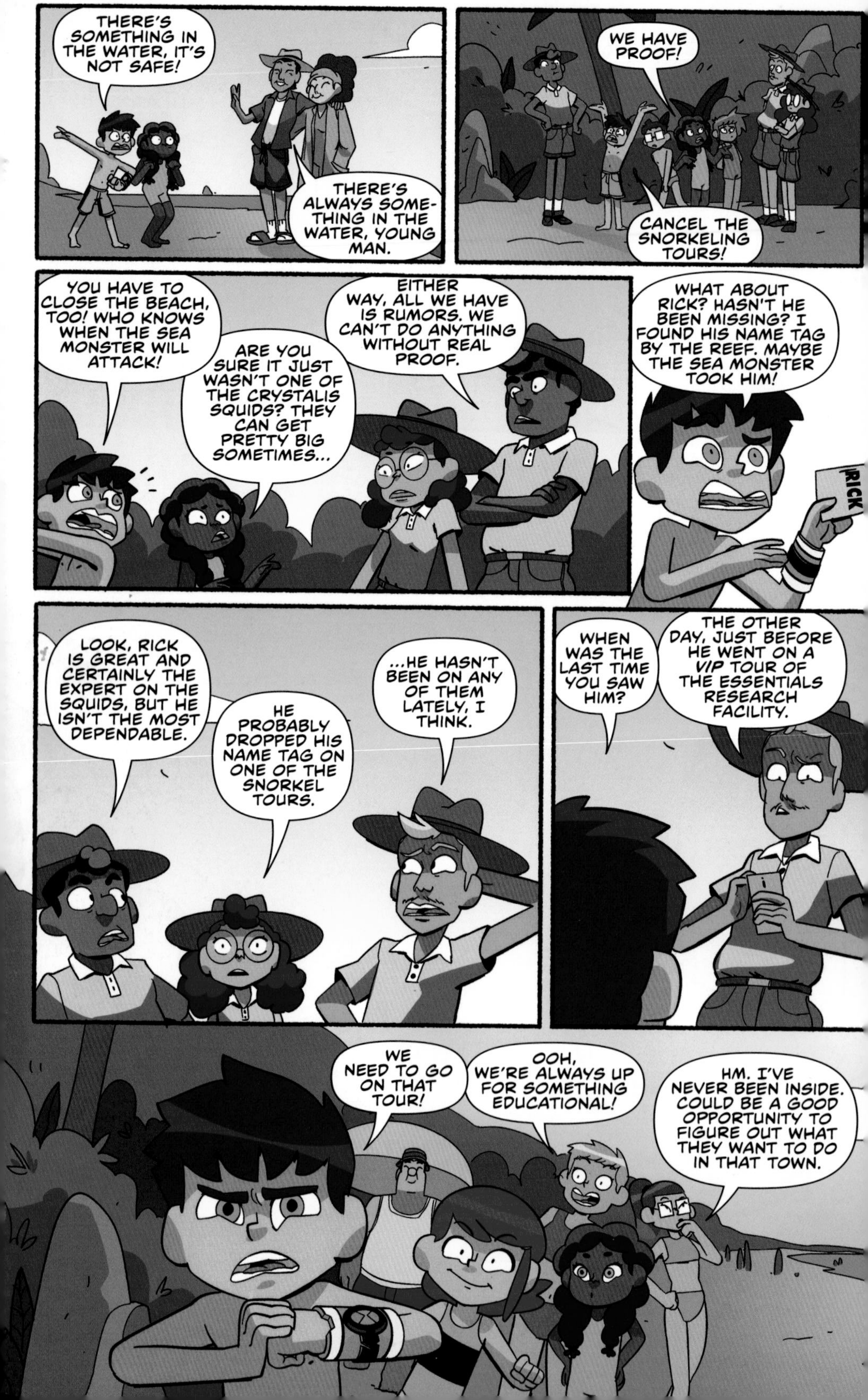
THERE'S SOMETHING IN THE WATER, IT'S NOT SAFE!
THERE'S ALWAYS SOME-THING IN THE WATER, YOUNG MAN.
WE HAVE PROOF!
CANCEL THE SNORKELING TOURS!
YOU HAVE TO CLOSE THE BEACH, TOO! WHO KNOWS WHEN THE SEA MONSTER WILL ATTACK!
ARE YOU SURE IT JUST WASN'T ONE OF THE CRYSTALIS SQUIDS? THEY CAN GET PRETTY BIG SOMETIMES...
EITHER WAY, ALL WE HAVE IS RUMORS. WE CAN'T DO ANYTHING WITHOUT REAL PROOF.
WHAT ABOUT RICK? HASN'T HE BEEN MISSING? I FOUND HIS NAME TAG BY THE REEF. MAYBE THE SEA MONSTER TOOK HIM!
RICK
LOOK, RICK IS GREAT AND CERTAINLY THE EXPERT ON THE SQUIDS, BUT HE ISN'T THE MOST DEPENDABLE.
HE PROBABLY DROPPED HIS NAME TAG ON ONE OF THE SNORKEL TOURS.
...HE HASN'T BEEN ON ANY OF THEM LATELY, I THINK.
WHEN WAS THE LAST TIME YOU SAW HIM?
THE OTHER DAY, JUST BEFORE HE WENT ON A *VIP* TOUR OF THE ESSENTIALS RESEARCH FACILITY.
WE NEED TO GO ON THAT TOUR!
OOH, WE'RE ALWAYS UP FOR SOMETHING EDUCATIONAL!
HM. I'VE NEVER BEEN INSIDE. COULD BE A GOOD OPPORTUNITY TO FIGURE OUT WHAT THEY WANT TO DO IN THAT TOWN.

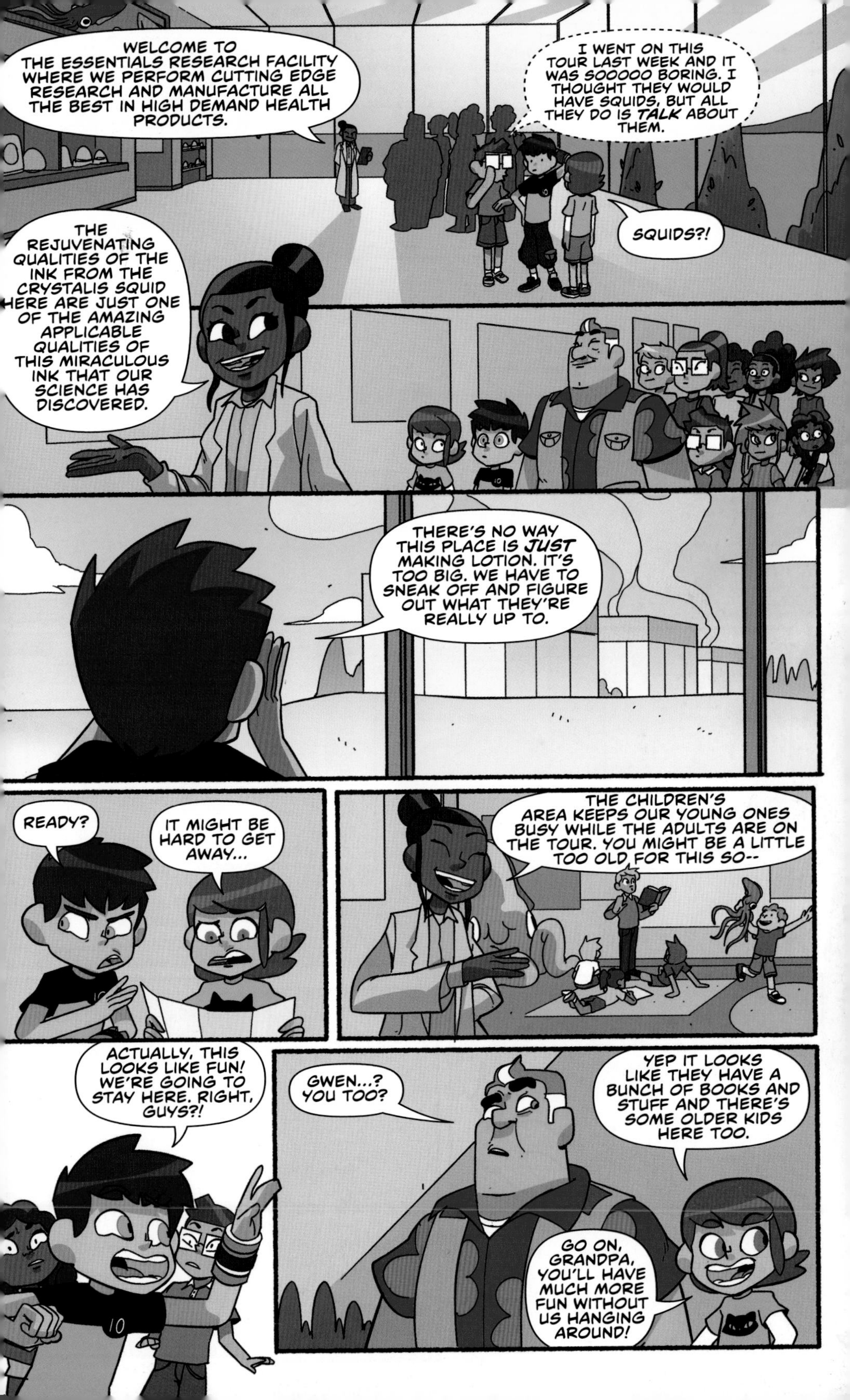
WELCOME TO THE ESSENTIALS RESEARCH FACILITY WHERE WE PERFORM CUTTING EDGE RESEARCH AND MANUFACTURE ALL THE BEST IN HIGH DEMAND HEALTH PRODUCTS.
I WENT ON THIS TOUR LAST WEEK AND IT WAS SOOOOO BORING. I THOUGHT THEY WOULD HAVE SQUIDS, BUT ALL THEY DO IS *TALK* ABOUT THEM.
SQUIDS?!
THE REJUVENATING QUALITIES OF THE INK FROM THE CRYSTALIS SQUID HERE ARE JUST ONE OF THE AMAZING APPLICABLE QUALITIES OF THIS MIRACULOUS INK THAT OUR SCIENCE HAS DISCOVERED.
THERE'S NO WAY THIS PLACE IS *JUST* MAKING LOTION. IT'S TOO BIG. WE HAVE TO SNEAK OFF AND FIGURE OUT WHAT THEY'RE REALLY UP TO.
READY?
IT MIGHT BE HARD TO GET AWAY...
THE CHILDREN'S AREA KEEPS OUR YOUNG ONES BUSY WHILE THE ADULTS ARE ON THE TOUR. YOU MIGHT BE A LITTLE TOO OLD FOR THIS SO--
ACTUALLY, THIS LOOKS LIKE FUN! WE'RE GOING TO STAY HERE. RIGHT, GUYS?!
GWEN...? YOU TOO?
YEP IT LOOKS LIKE THEY HAVE A BUNCH OF BOOKS AND STUFF AND THERE'S SOME OLDER KIDS HERE TOO.
GO ON, GRANDPA, YOU'LL HAVE MUCH MORE FUN WITHOUT US HANGING AROUND!

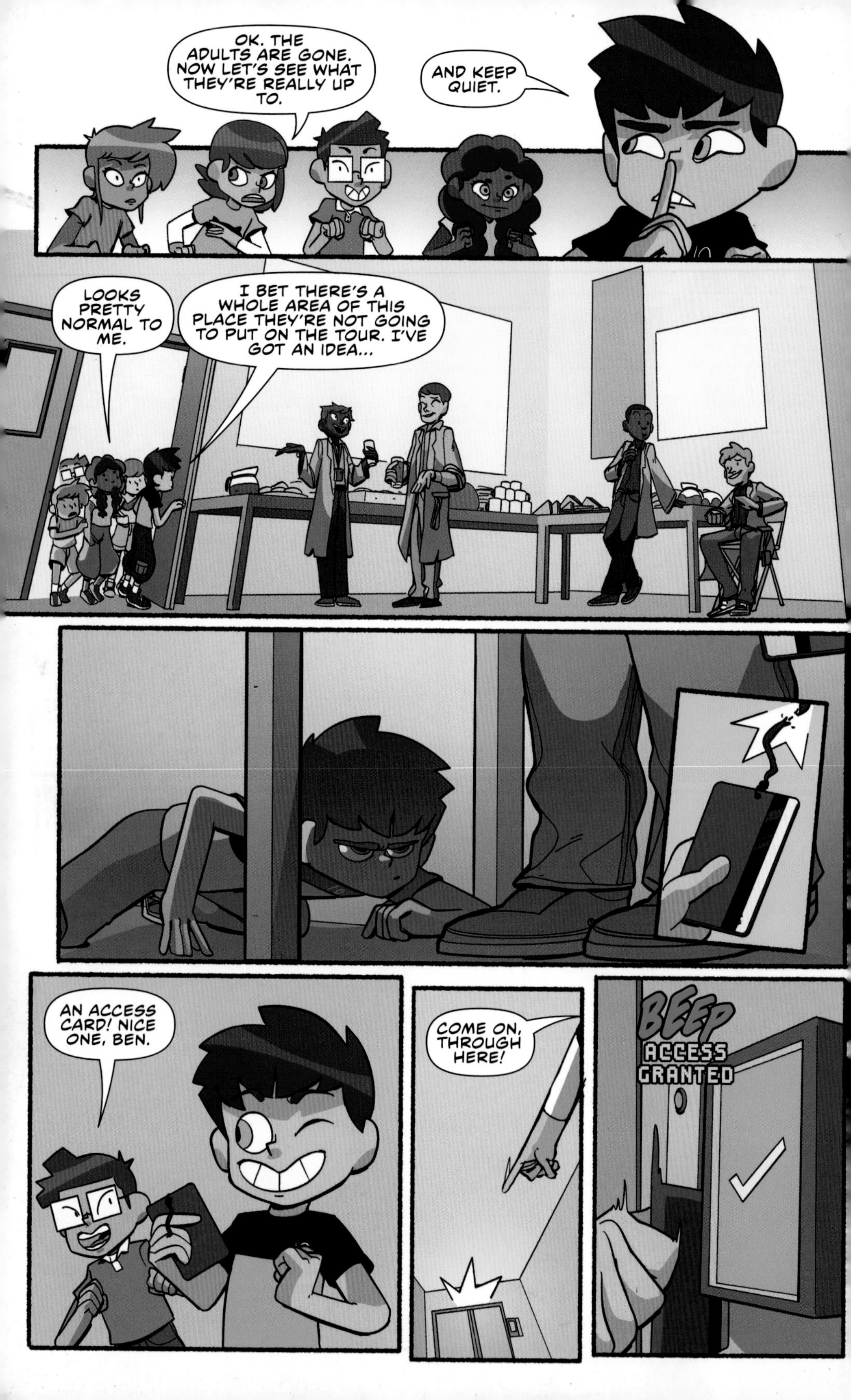
OK. THE ADULTS ARE GONE. NOW LET'S SEE WHAT THEY'RE REALLY UP TO.
AND KEEP QUIET.
LOOKS PRETTY NORMAL TO ME.
I BET THERE'S A WHOLE AREA OF THIS PLACE THEY'RE NOT GOING TO PUT ON THE TOUR. I'VE GOT AN IDEA...
AN ACCESS CARD! NICE ONE, BEN.
COME ON, THROUGH HERE!
BEEP
ACCESS GRANTED

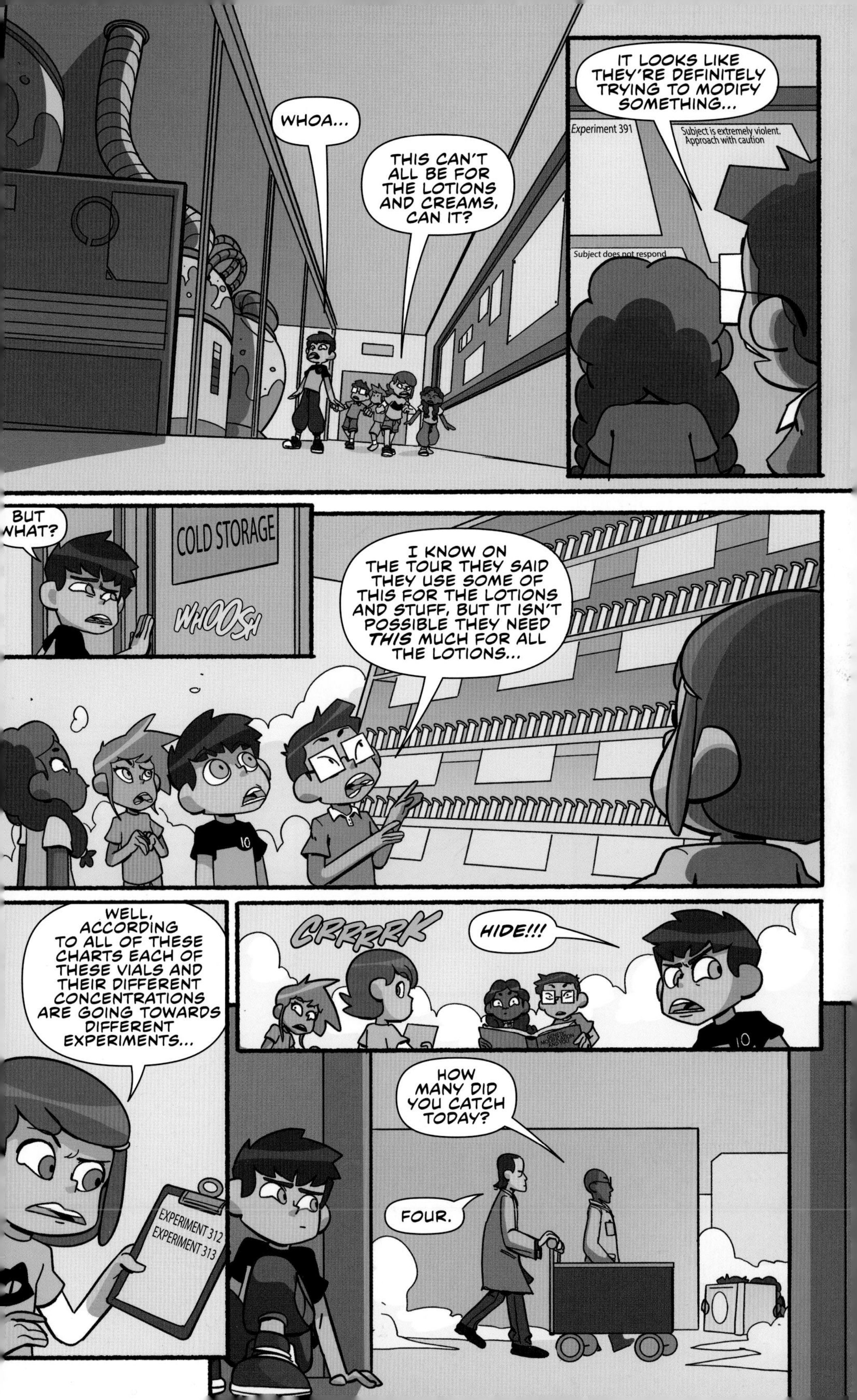
WHOA...
THIS CAN'T ALL BE FOR THE LOTIONS AND CREAMS, CAN IT?
IT LOOKS LIKE THEY'RE DEFINITELY TRYING TO MODIFY SOMETHING...
Experiment 391
Subject is extremely violent. Approach with caution
Subject does not respond
BUT WHAT?
COLD STORAGE
WHOOSH
I KNOW ON THE TOUR THEY SAID THEY USE SOME OF THIS FOR THE LOTIONS AND STUFF, BUT IT ISN'T POSSIBLE THEY NEED THIS MUCH FOR ALL THE LOTIONS...
WELL, ACCORDING TO ALL OF THESE CHARTS EACH OF THESE VIALS AND THEIR DIFFERENT CONCENTRATIONS ARE GOING TOWARDS DIFFERENT EXPERIMENTS...
EXPERIMENT 312
EXPERIMENT 313
CRRRRK
HIDE!!!
HOW MANY DID YOU CATCH TODAY?
FOUR.

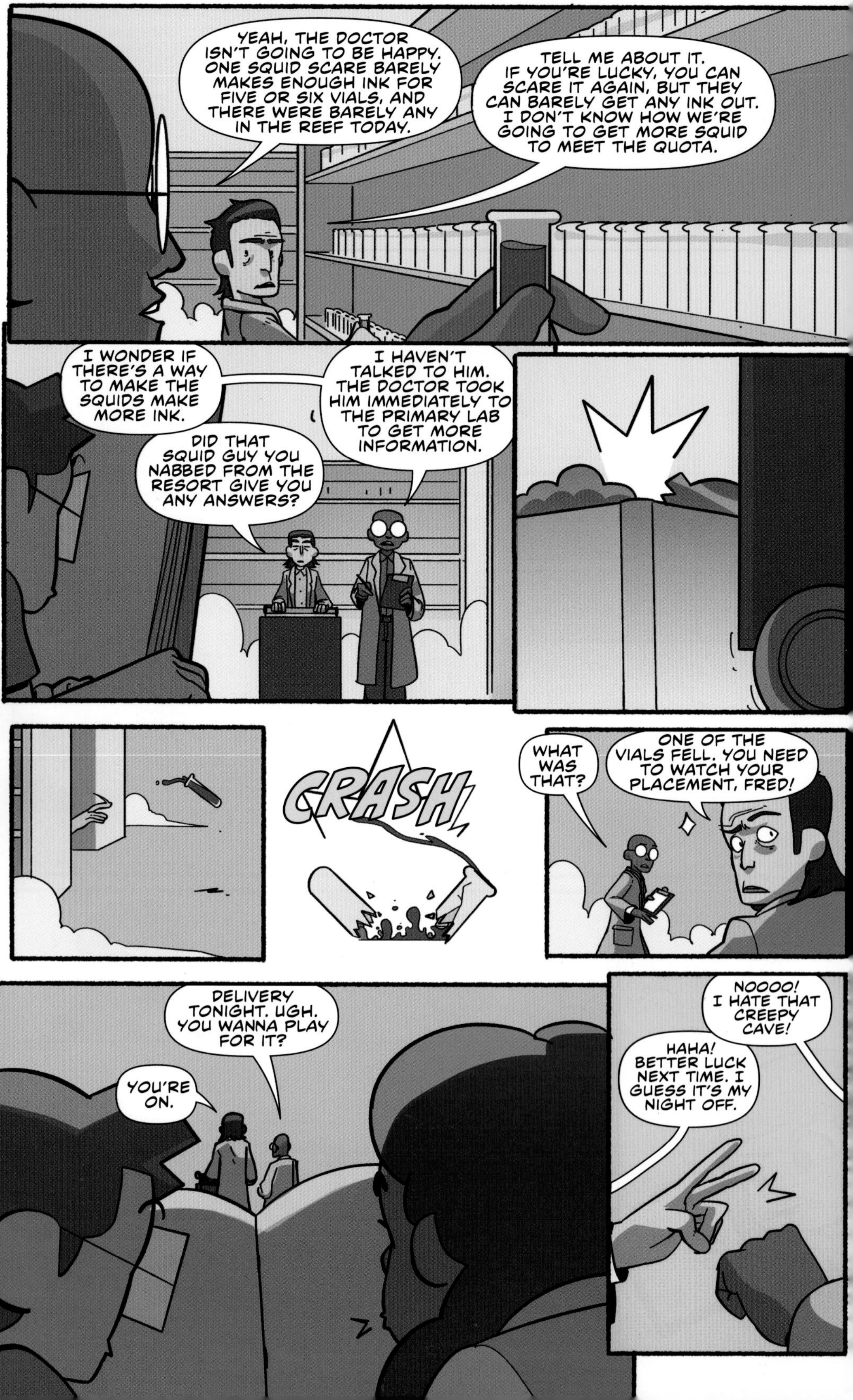
YEAH, THE DOCTOR ISN'T GOING TO BE HAPPY. ONE SQUID SCARE BARELY MAKES ENOUGH INK FOR FIVE OR SIX VIALS, AND THERE WERE BARELY ANY IN THE REEF TODAY.
TELL ME ABOUT IT. IF YOU'RE LUCKY, YOU CAN SCARE IT AGAIN, BUT THEY CAN BARELY GET ANY INK OUT. I DON'T KNOW HOW WE'RE GOING TO GET MORE SQUID TO MEET THE QUOTA.
I WONDER IF THERE'S A WAY TO MAKE THE SQUIDS MAKE MORE INK.
DID THAT SQUID GUY YOU NABBED FROM THE RESORT GIVE YOU ANY ANSWERS?
I HAVEN'T TALKED TO HIM. THE DOCTOR TOOK HIM IMMEDIATELY TO THE PRIMARY LAB TO GET MORE INFORMATION.
CRASH
WHAT WAS THAT?
ONE OF THE VIALS FELL. YOU NEED TO WATCH YOUR PLACEMENT, FRED!
DELIVERY TONIGHT. UGH. YOU WANNA PLAY FOR IT?
YOU'RE ON.
NOOOO! I HATE THAT CREEPY CAVE!
HAHA! BETTER LUCK NEXT TIME. I GUESS IT'S MY NIGHT OFF.

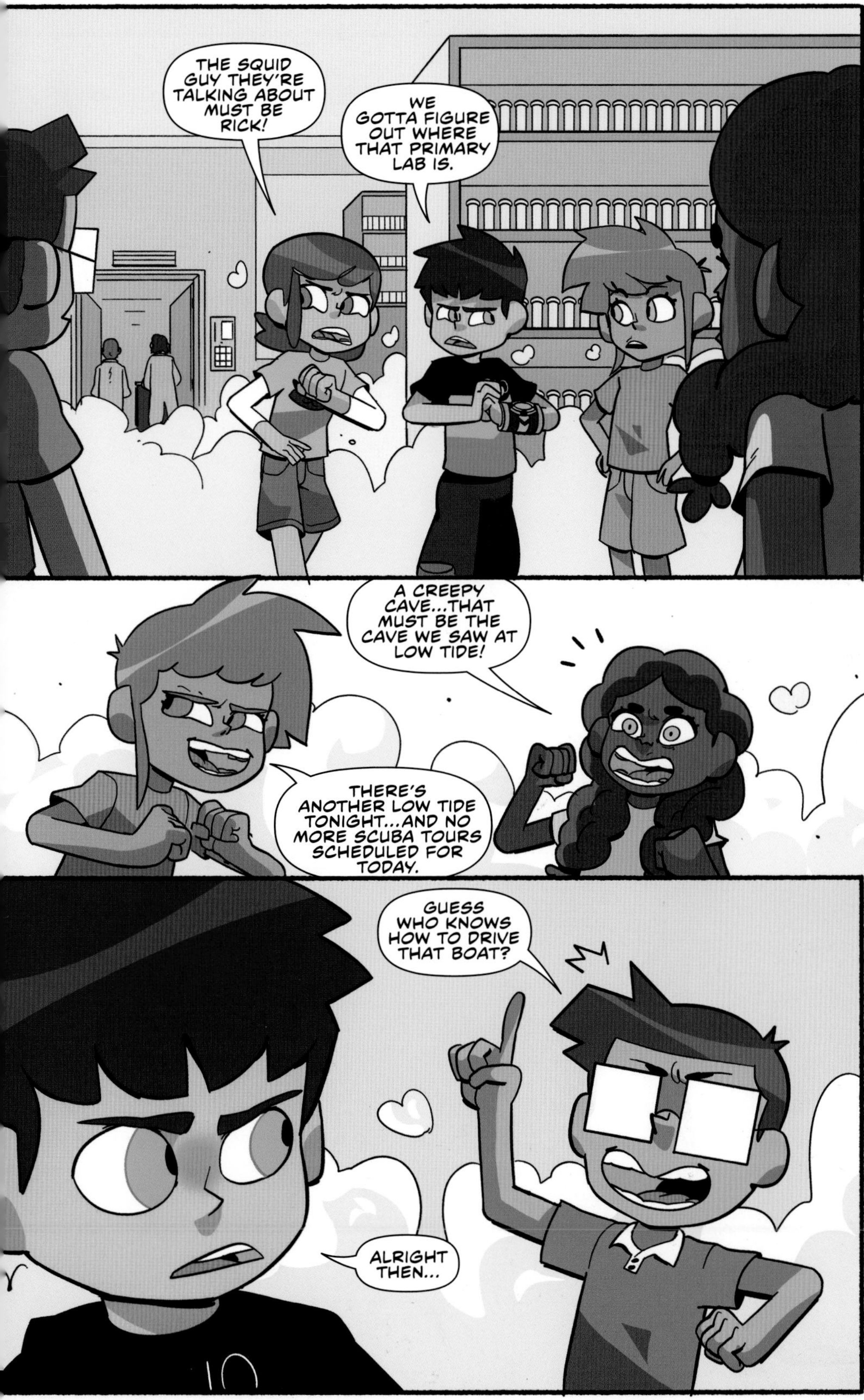
THE SQUID GUY THEY'RE TALKING ABOUT MUST BE RICK!
WE GOTTA FIGURE OUT WHERE THAT PRIMARY LAB IS.
A CREEPY CAVE...THAT MUST BE THE CAVE WE SAW AT LOW TIDE!
THERE'S ANOTHER LOW TIDE TONIGHT...AND NO MORE SCUBA TOURS SCHEDULED FOR TODAY.
GUESS WHO KNOWS HOW TO DRIVE THAT BOAT?
ALRIGHT THEN...

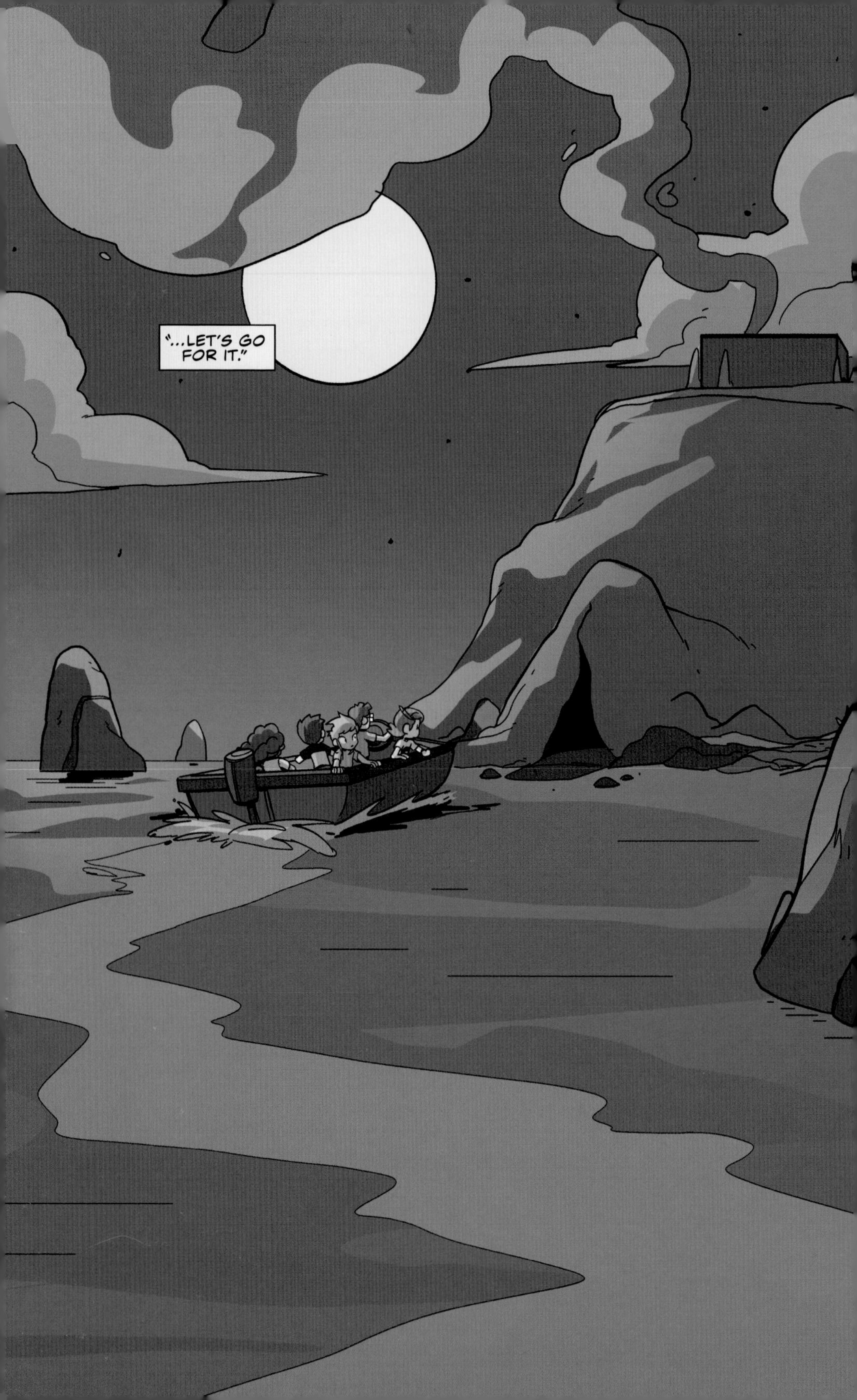
"...LET'S GO FOR IT."

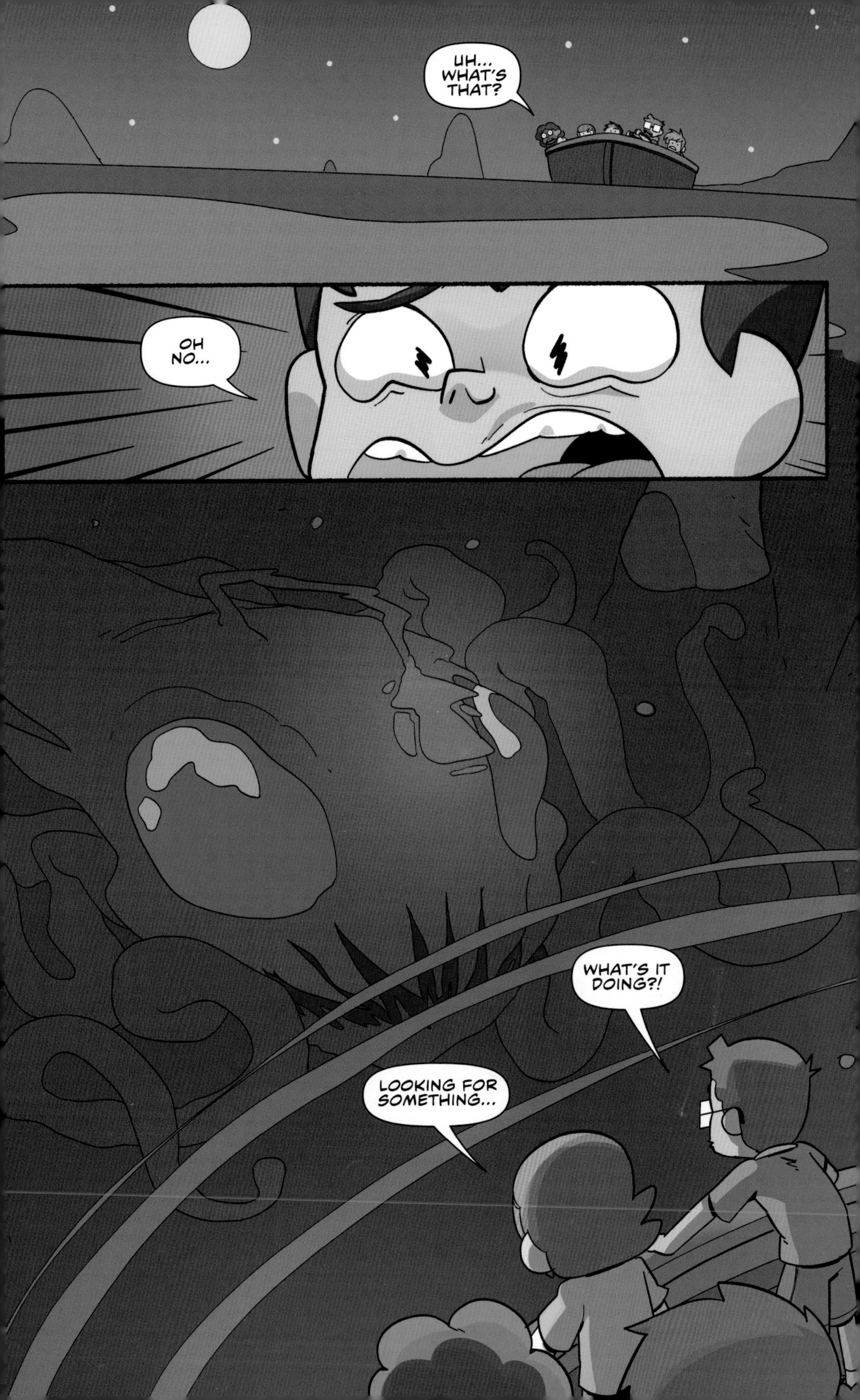
UH... WHAT'S THAT?
OH NO...
WHAT'S IT DOING?!
LOOKING FOR SOMETHING...

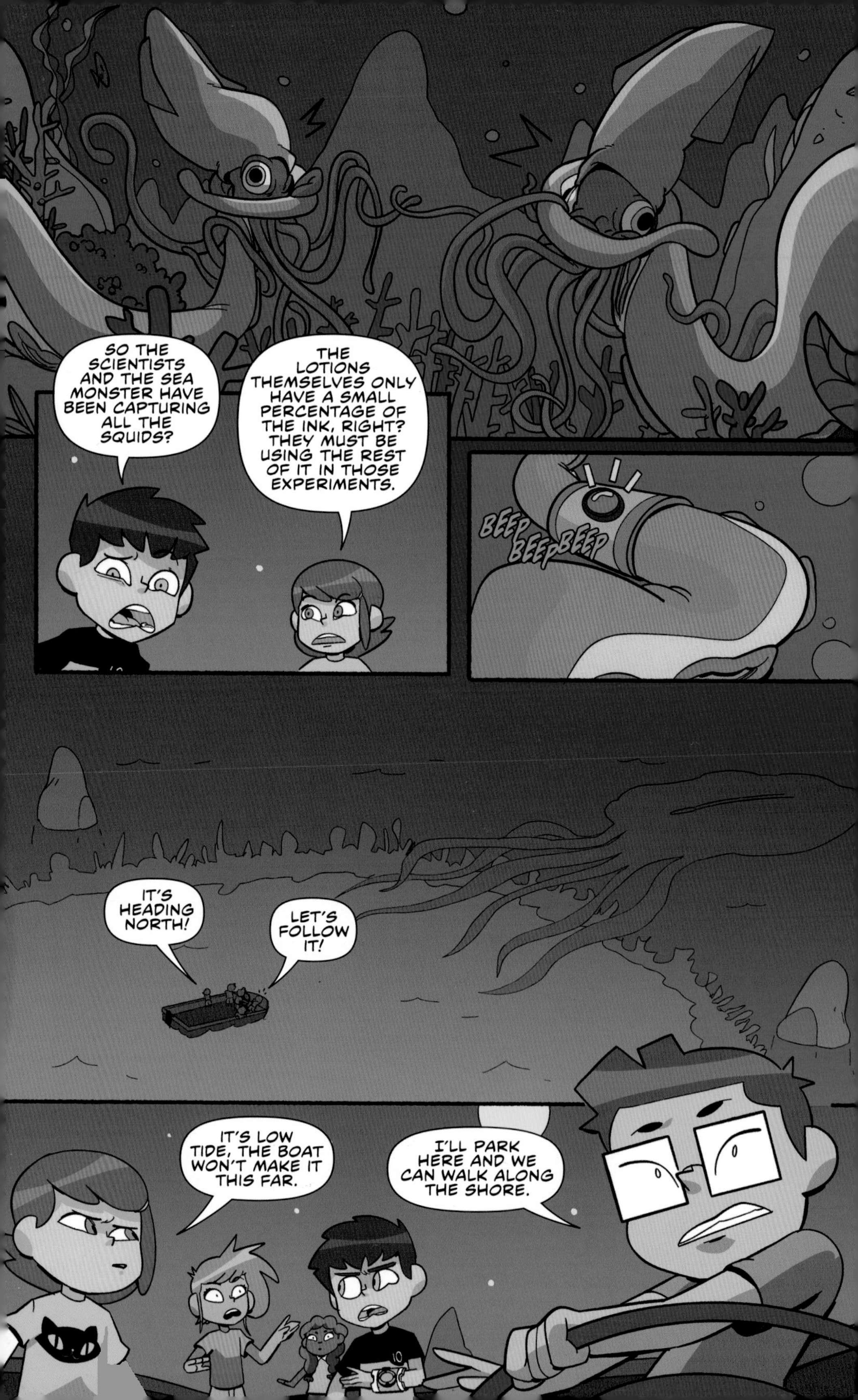
SO THE SCIENTISTS AND THE SEA MONSTER HAVE BEEN CAPTURING ALL THE SQUIDS?
THE LOTIONS THEMSELVES ONLY HAVE A SMALL PERCENTAGE OF THE INK, RIGHT? THEY MUST BE USING THE REST OF IT IN THOSE EXPERIMENTS.
BEEP BEEP BEEP
IT'S HEADING NORTH!
LET'S FOLLOW IT!
IT'S LOW TIDE, THE BOAT WON'T MAKE IT THIS FAR.
I'LL PARK HERE AND WE CAN WALK ALONG THE SHORE.

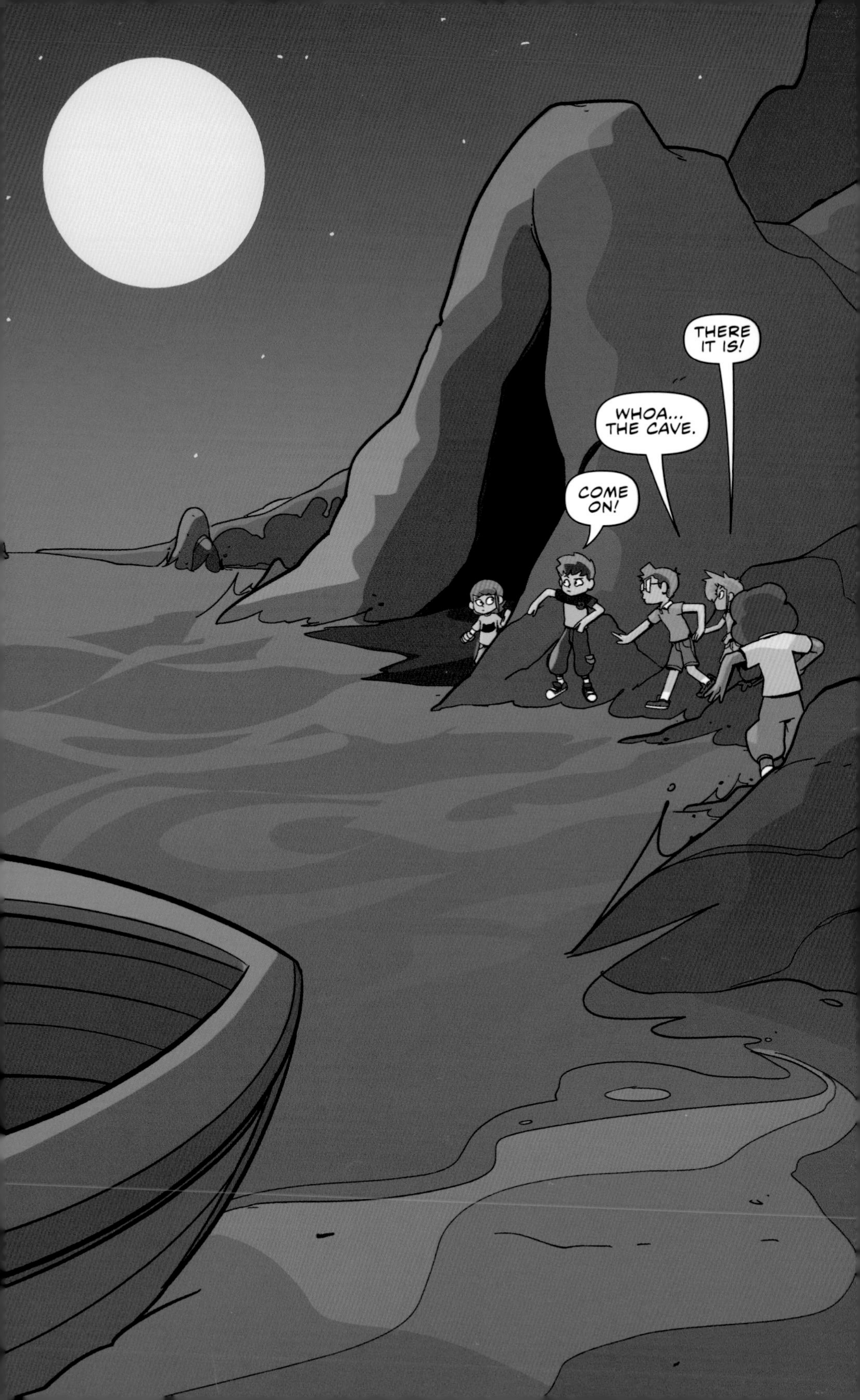
THERE IT IS!
WHOA... THE CAVE.
COME ON!

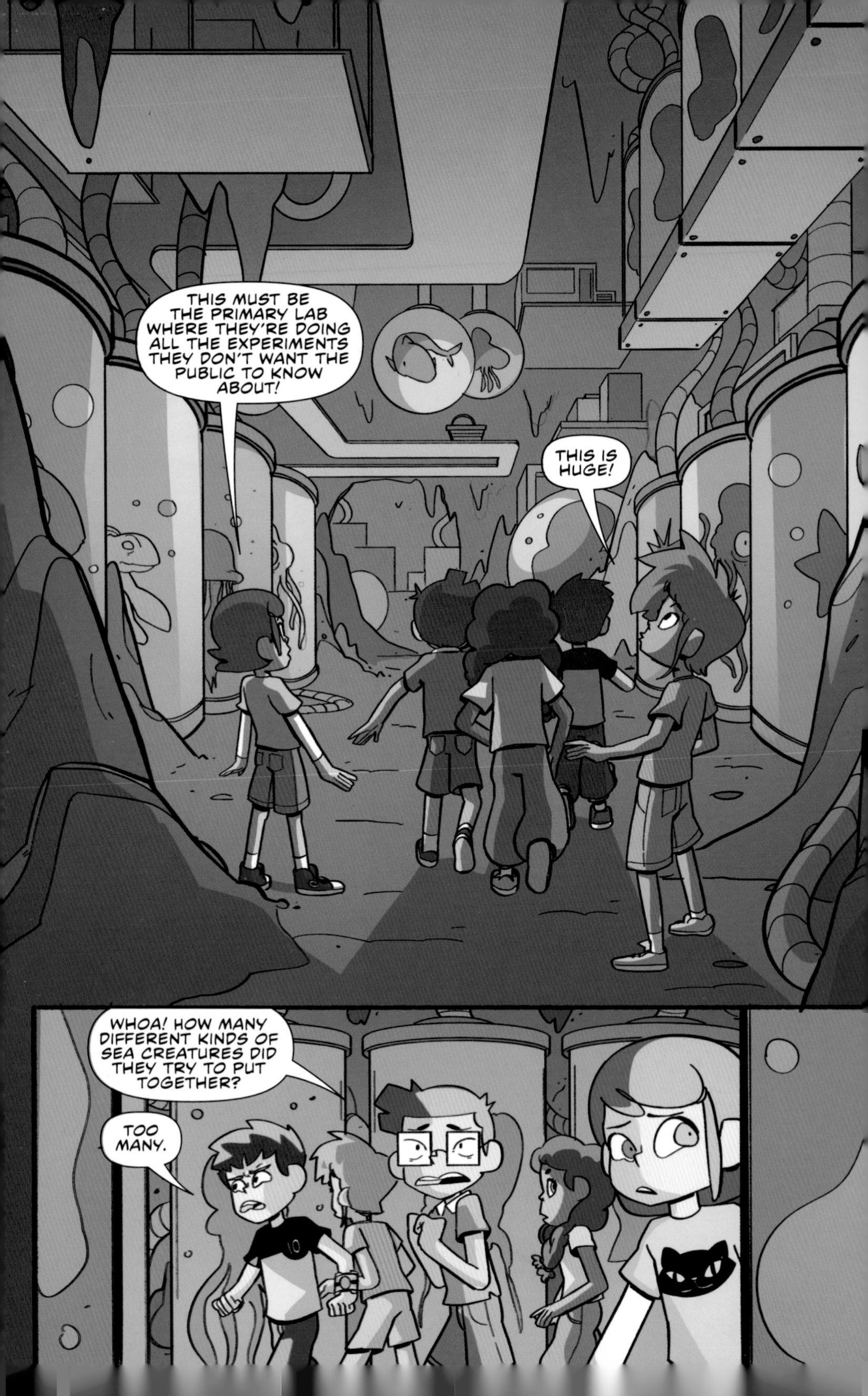
THIS MUST BE THE PRIMARY LAB WHERE THEY'RE DOING ALL THE EXPERIMENTS THEY DON'T WANT THE PUBLIC TO KNOW ABOUT!
THIS IS HUGE!
WHOA! HOW MANY DIFFERENT KINDS OF SEA CREATURES DID THEY TRY TO PUT TOGETHER?
TOO MANY.

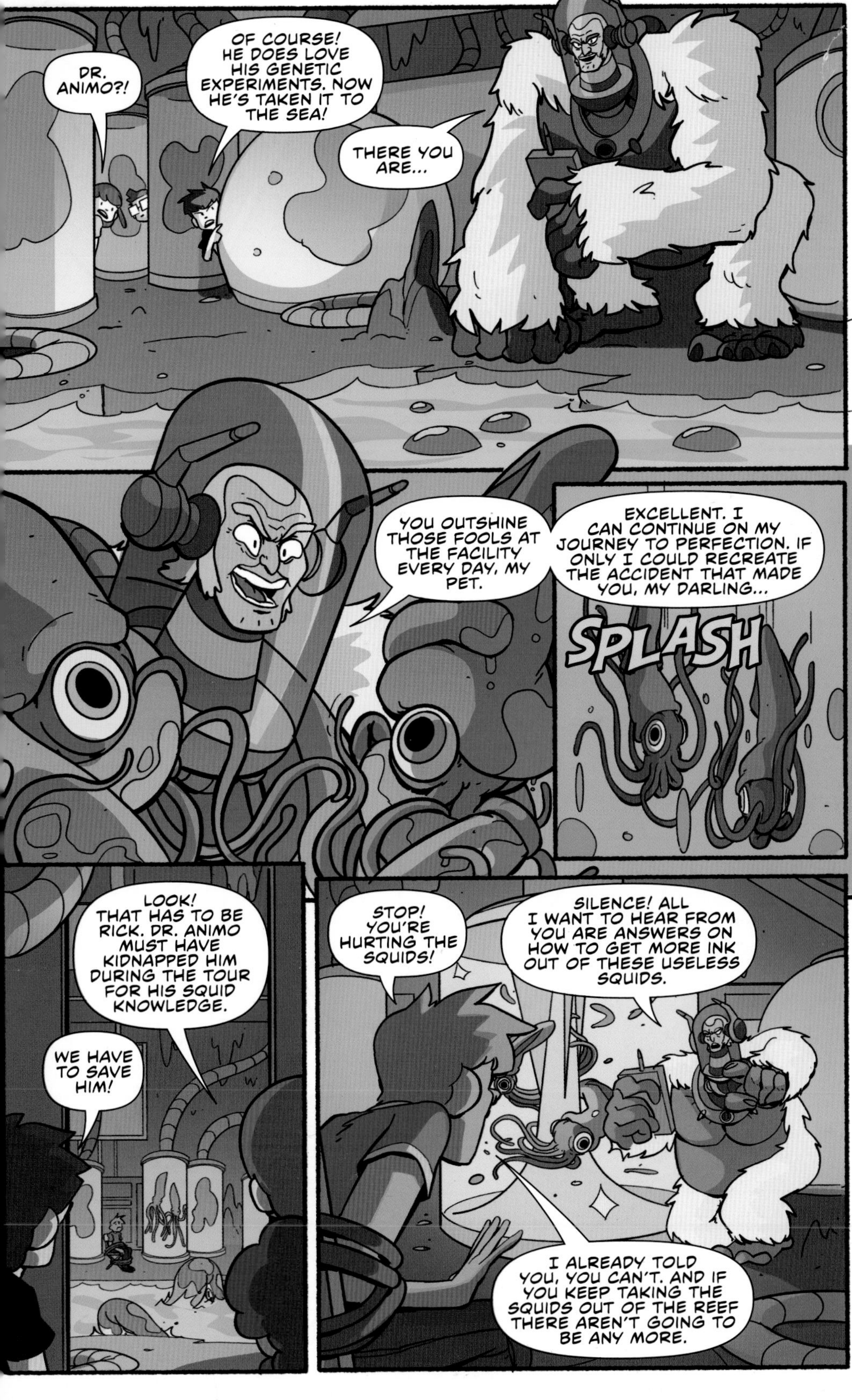
DR. ANIMO?!
OF COURSE! HE DOES LOVE HIS GENETIC EXPERIMENTS. NOW HE'S TAKEN IT TO THE SEA!
THERE YOU ARE...
YOU OUTSHINE THOSE FOOLS AT THE FACILITY EVERY DAY, MY PET.
EXCELLENT. I CAN CONTINUE ON MY JOURNEY TO PERFECTION. IF ONLY I COULD RECREATE THE ACCIDENT THAT MADE YOU, MY DARLING...
SPLASH
LOOK! THAT HAS TO BE RICK. DR. ANIMO MUST HAVE KIDNAPPED HIM DURING THE TOUR FOR HIS SQUID KNOWLEDGE.
WE HAVE TO SAVE HIM!
STOP! YOU'RE HURTING THE SQUIDS!
SILENCE! ALL I WANT TO HEAR FROM YOU ARE ANSWERS ON HOW TO GET MORE INK OUT OF THESE USELESS SQUIDS.
I ALREADY TOLD YOU, YOU CAN'T. AND IF YOU KEEP TAKING THE SQUIDS OUT OF THE REEF THERE AREN'T GOING TO BE ANY MORE.

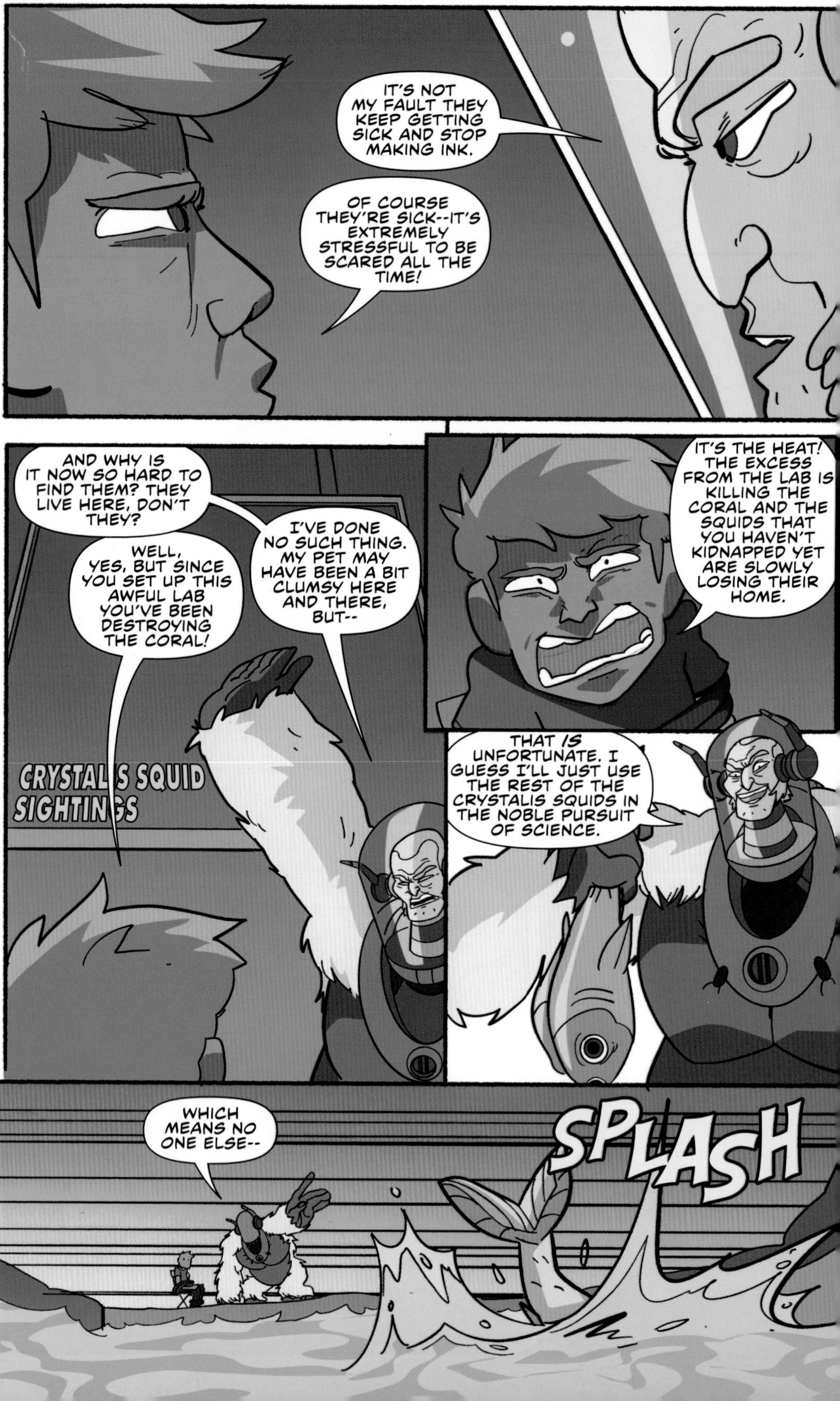
IT'S NOT MY FAULT THEY KEEP GETTING SICK AND STOP MAKING INK.
OF COURSE THEY'RE SICK--IT'S EXTREMELY STRESSFUL TO BE SCARED ALL THE TIME!
AND WHY IS IT NOW SO HARD TO FIND THEM? THEY LIVE HERE, DON'T THEY?
WELL, YES, BUT SINCE YOU SET UP THIS AWFUL LAB YOU'VE BEEN DESTROYING THE CORAL!
I'VE DONE NO SUCH THING. MY PET MAY HAVE BEEN A BIT CLUMSY HERE AND THERE, BUT--
CRYSTALIS SQUID SIGHTINGS
IT'S THE HEAT! THE EXCESS FROM THE LAB IS KILLING THE CORAL AND THE SQUIDS THAT YOU HAVEN'T KIDNAPPED YET ARE SLOWLY LOSING THEIR HOME.
THAT *IS* UNFORTUNATE. I GUESS I'LL JUST USE THE REST OF THE CRYSTALIS SQUIDS IN THE NOBLE PURSUIT OF SCIENCE.
WHICH MEANS NO ONE ELSE--
SPLASH

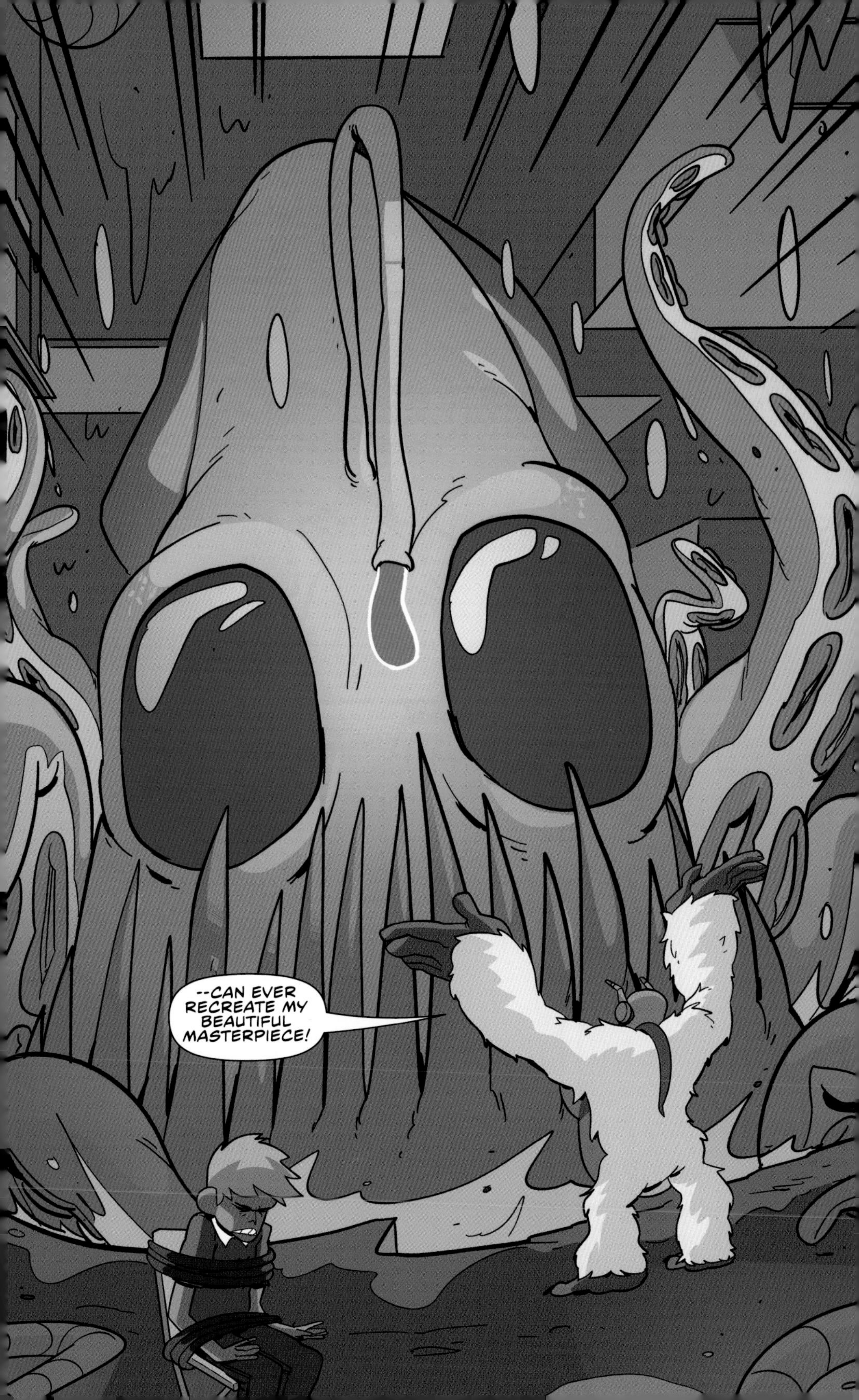
--CAN EVER RECREATE MY BEAUTIFUL MASTERPIECE!

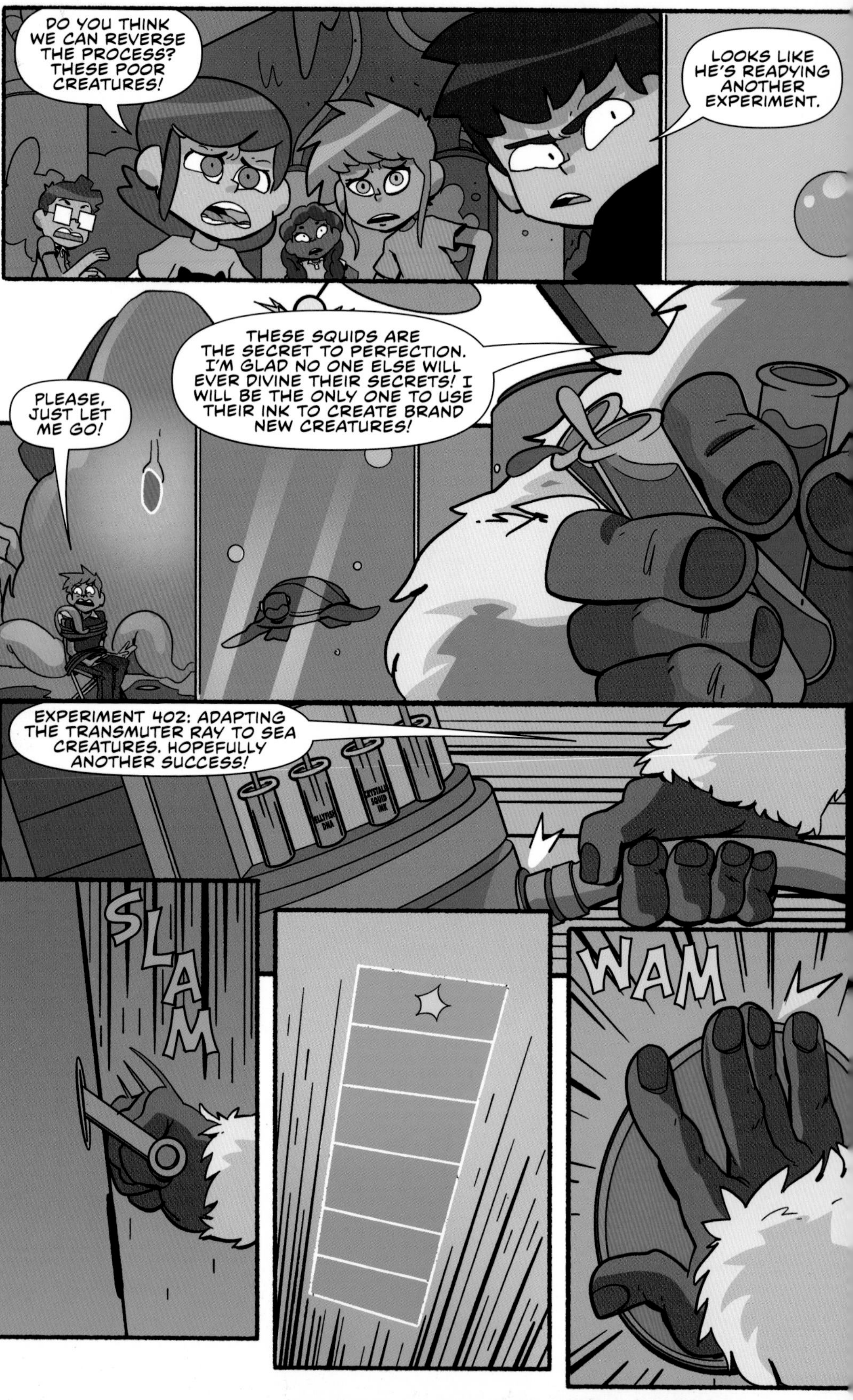
DO YOU THINK WE CAN REVERSE THE PROCESS? THESE POOR CREATURES!
LOOKS LIKE HE'S READYING ANOTHER EXPERIMENT.
THESE SQUIDS ARE THE SECRET TO PERFECTION. I'M GLAD NO ONE ELSE WILL EVER DIVINE THEIR SECRETS! I WILL BE THE ONLY ONE TO USE THEIR INK TO CREATE BRAND NEW CREATURES!
PLEASE, JUST LET ME GO!
EXPERIMENT 402: ADAPTING THE TRANSMUTER RAY TO SEA CREATURES. HOPEFULLY ANOTHER SUCCESS!
DNA
SQUID INK
SLAM
WAM

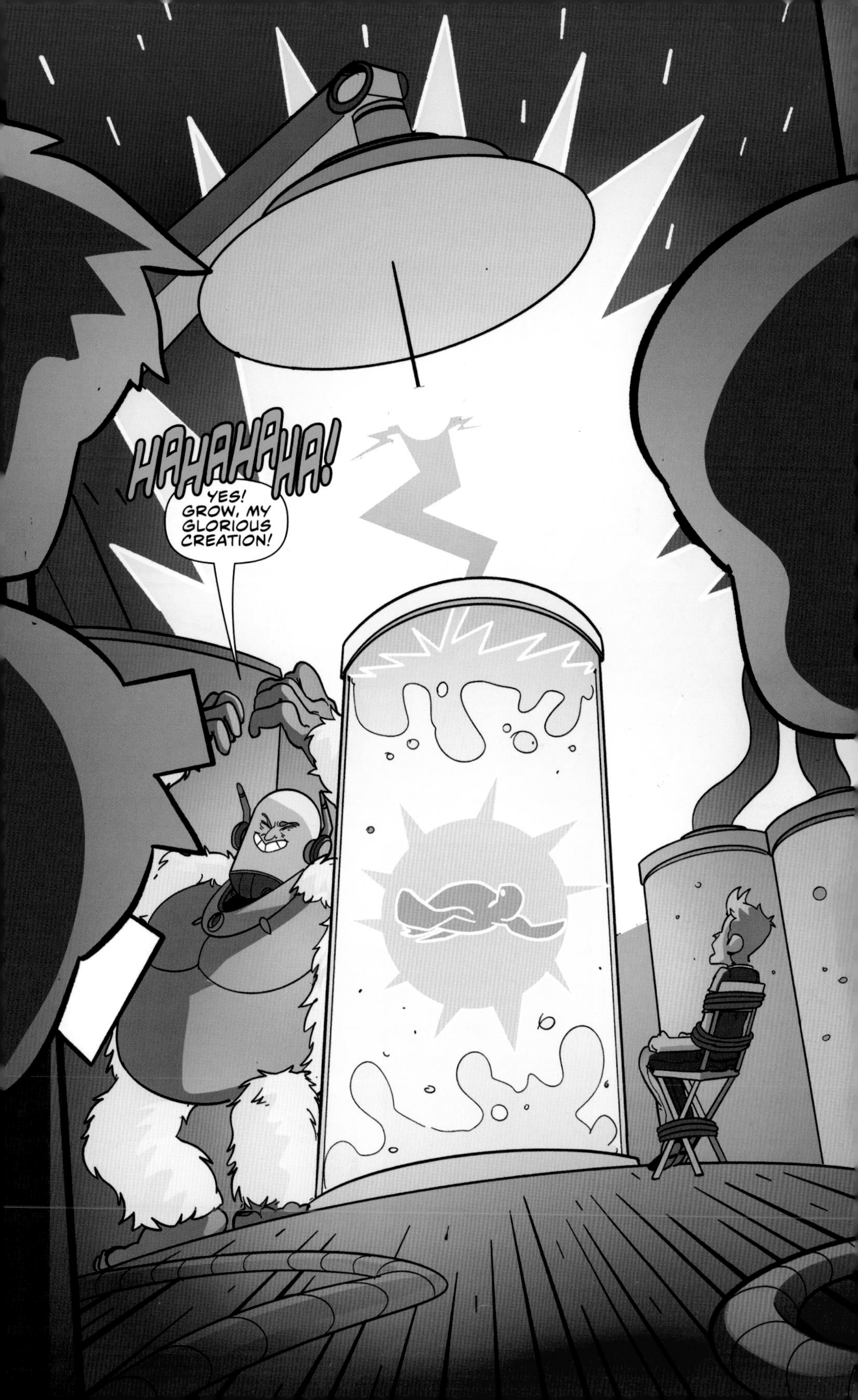
HAHAHAHAHA!
YES! GROW, MY GLORIOUS CREATION!

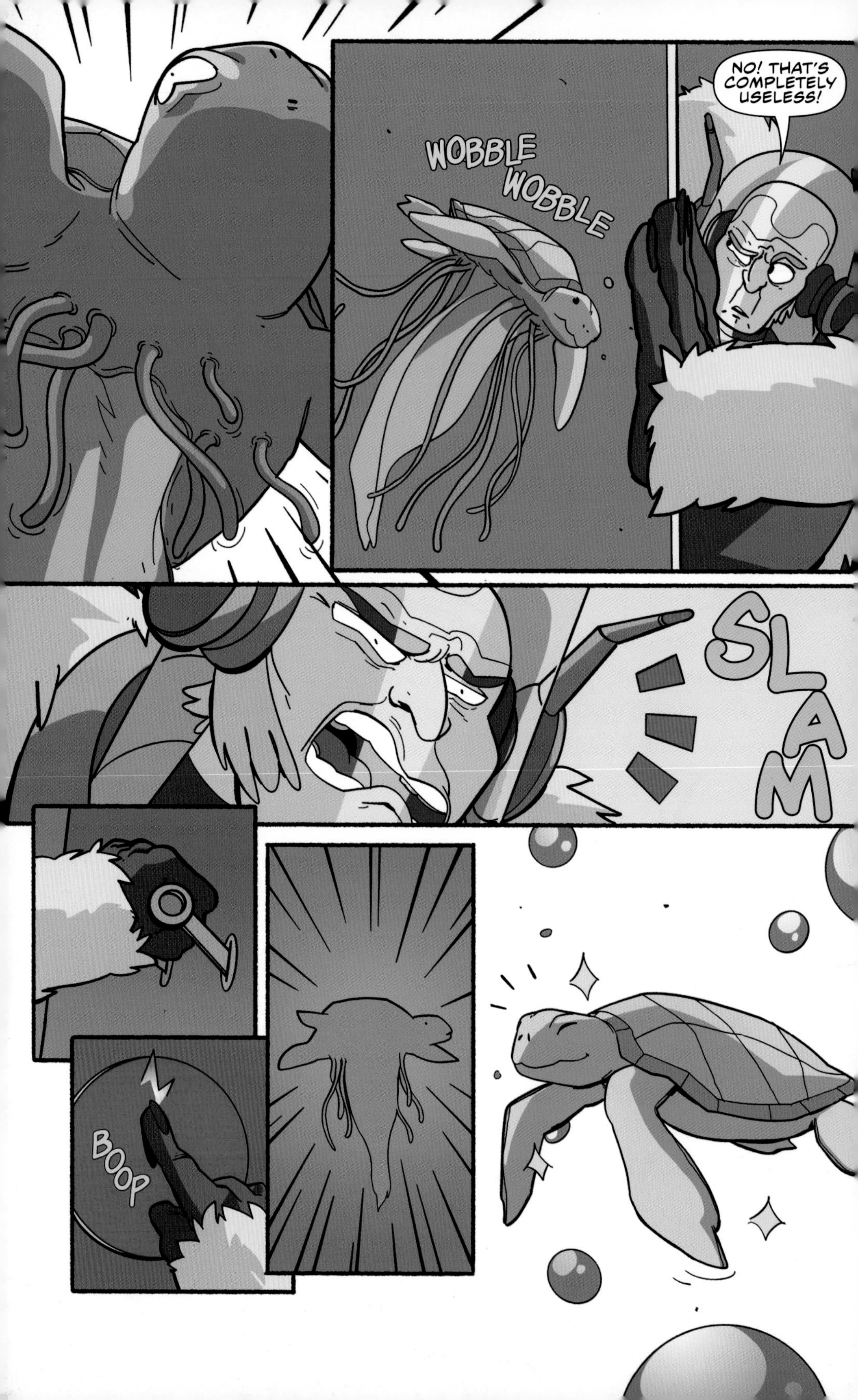

NO! THAT'S COMPLETELY USELESS!
WOBBLE WOBBLE
SLAM
BOOP

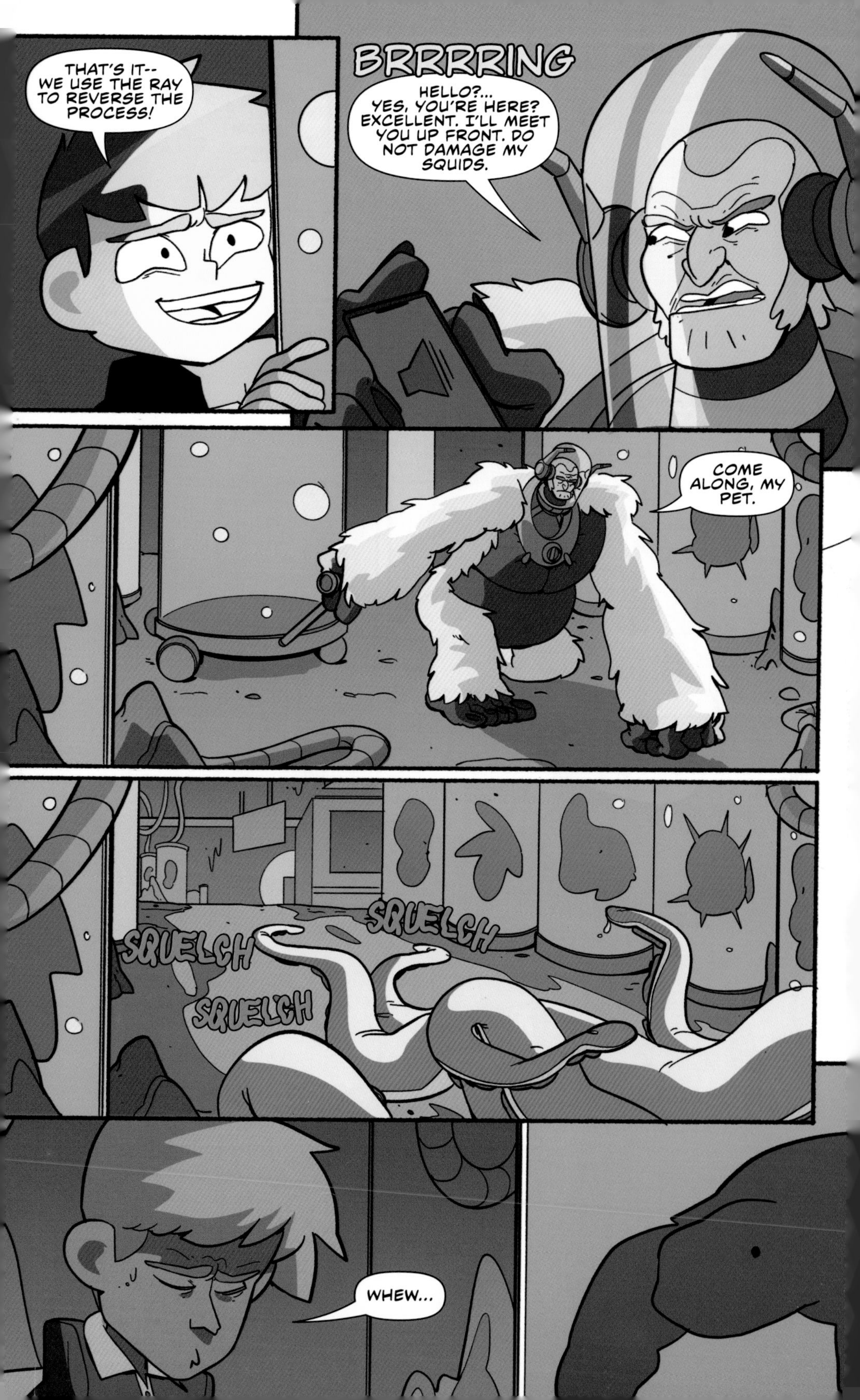
THAT'S IT-- WE USE THE RAY TO REVERSE THE PROCESS!
BRRRRING
HELLO?... YES, YOU'RE HERE? EXCELLENT. I'LL MEET YOU UP FRONT. DO NOT DAMAGE MY SQUIDS.
COME ALONG, MY PET.
SQUELCH
SQUELCH
SQUELCH
WHEW...

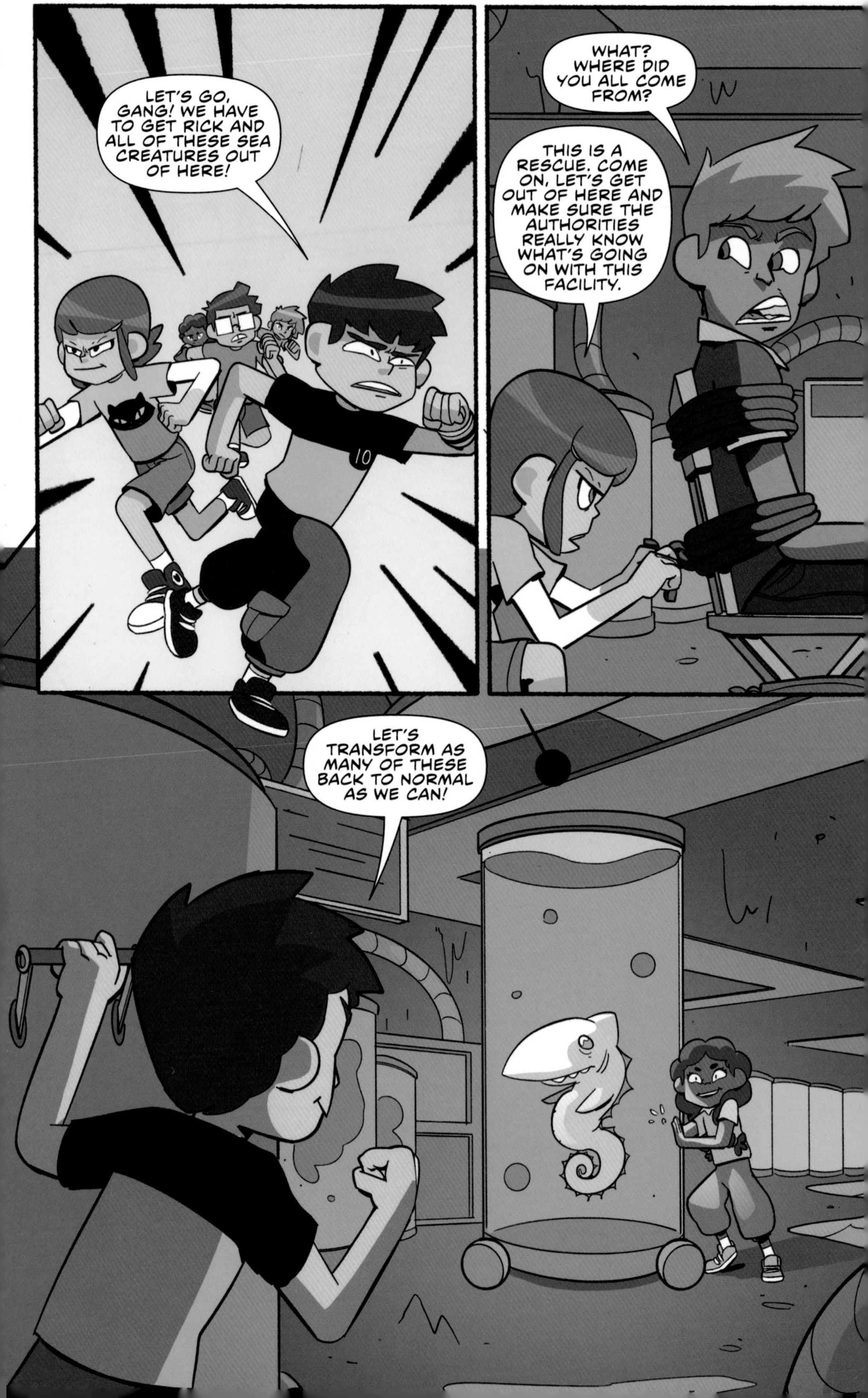
LET'S GO, GANG! WE HAVE TO GET RICK AND ALL OF THESE SEA CREATURES OUT OF HERE!
10
WHAT? WHERE DID YOU ALL COME FROM?
THIS IS A RESCUE. COME ON, LET'S GET OUT OF HERE AND MAKE SURE THE AUTHORITIES REALLY KNOW WHAT'S GOING ON WITH THIS FACILITY.
LET'S TRANSFORM AS MANY OF THESE BACK TO NORMAL AS WE CAN!

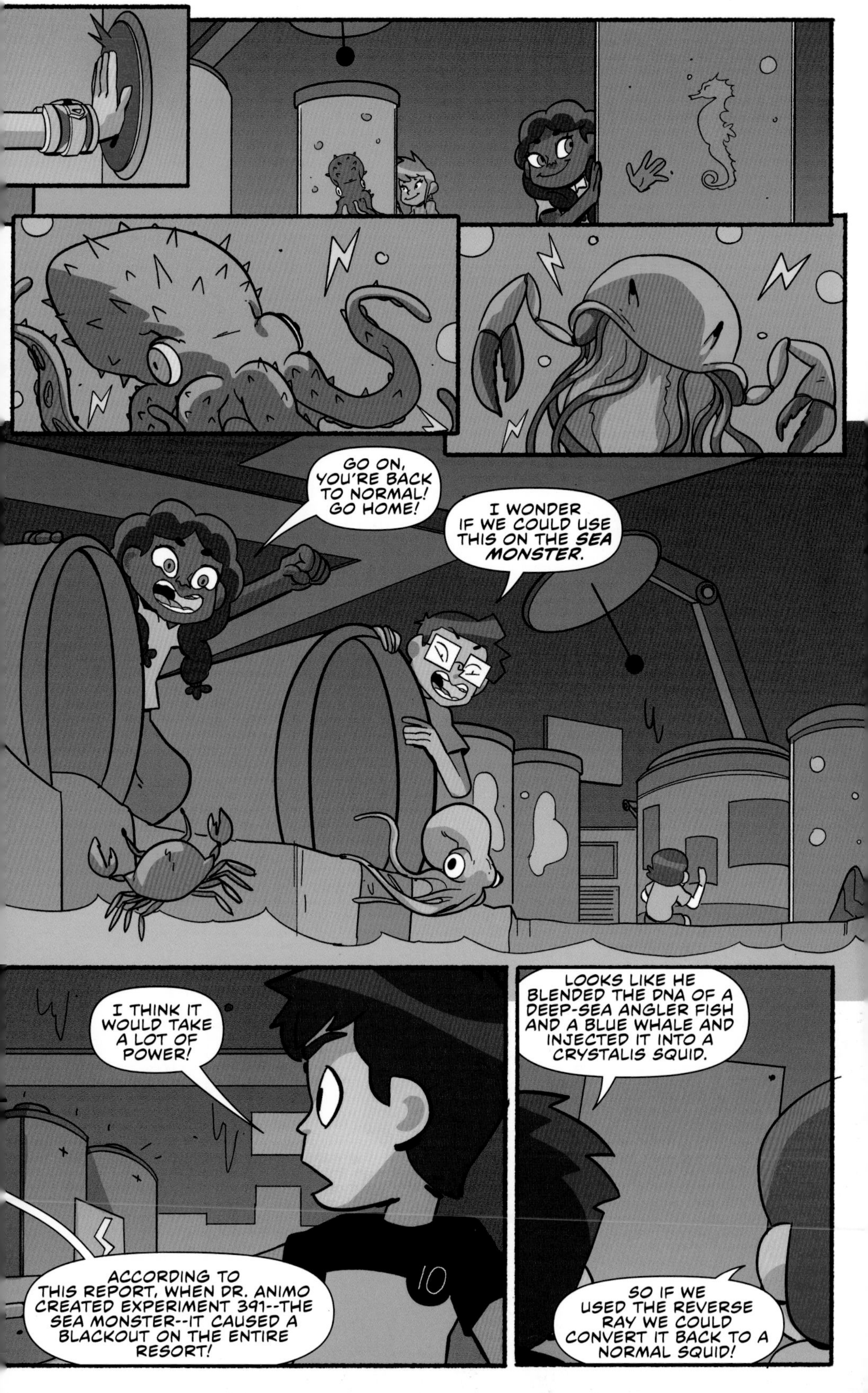
GO ON, YOU'RE BACK TO NORMAL! GO HOME!
I WONDER IF WE COULD USE THIS ON THE SEA MONSTER.
I THINK IT WOULD TAKE A LOT OF POWER!
ACCORDING TO THIS REPORT, WHEN DR. ANIMO CREATED EXPERIMENT 391--THE SEA MONSTER--IT CAUSED A BLACKOUT ON THE ENTIRE RESORT!
10
LOOKS LIKE HE BLENDED THE DNA OF A DEEP-SEA ANGLER FISH AND A BLUE WHALE AND INJECTED IT INTO A CRYSTALIS SQUID.
SO IF WE USED THE REVERSE RAY WE COULD CONVERT IT BACK TO A NORMAL SQUID!

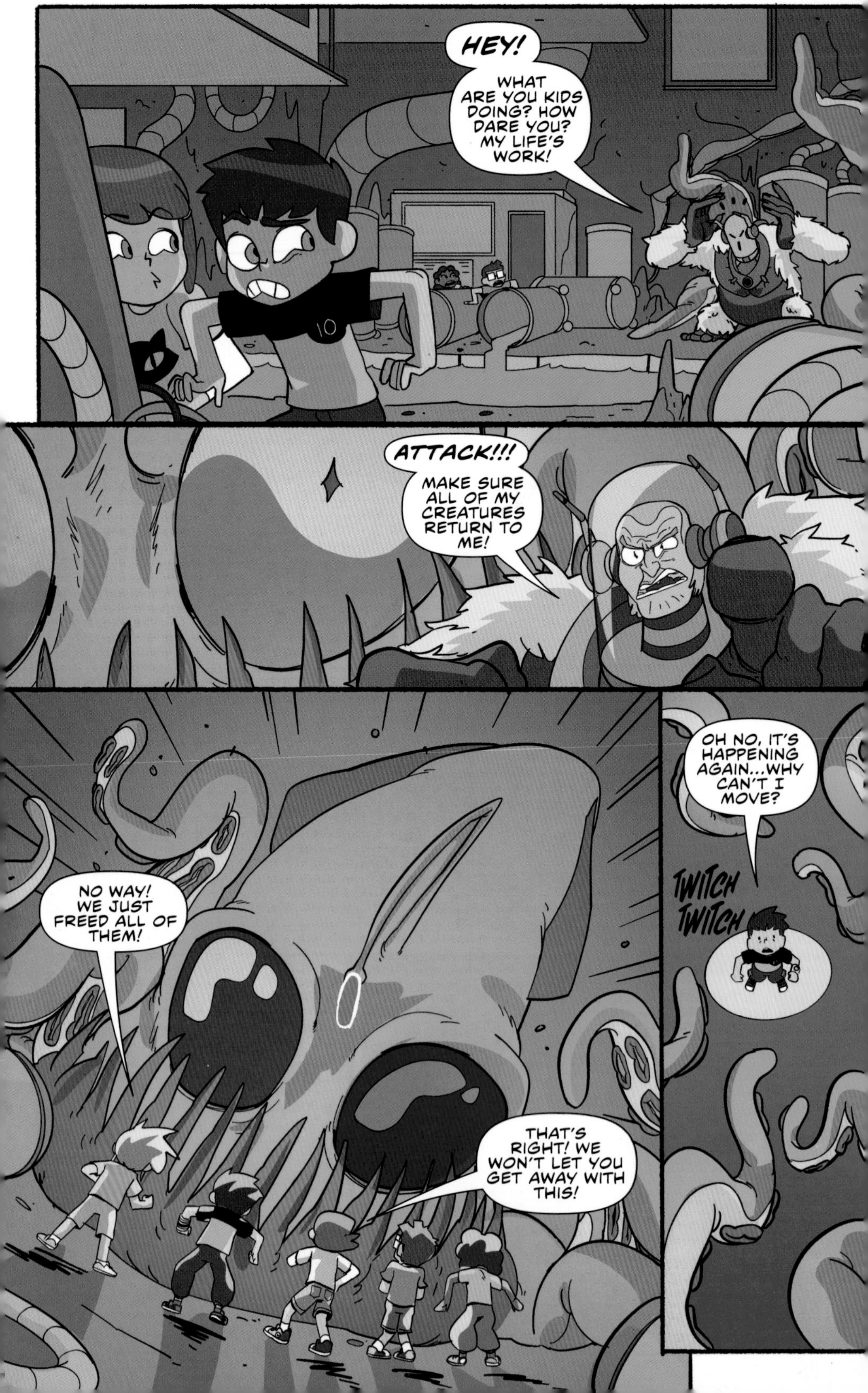
HEY!
WHAT ARE YOU KIDS DOING? HOW DARE YOU? MY LIFE'S WORK!
ATTACK!!!
MAKE SURE ALL OF MY CREATURES RETURN TO ME!
NO WAY! WE JUST FREED ALL OF THEM!
THAT'S RIGHT! WE WON'T LET YOU GET AWAY WITH THIS!
OH NO, IT'S HAPPENING AGAIN...WHY CAN'T I MOVE?
TWITCH TWITCH

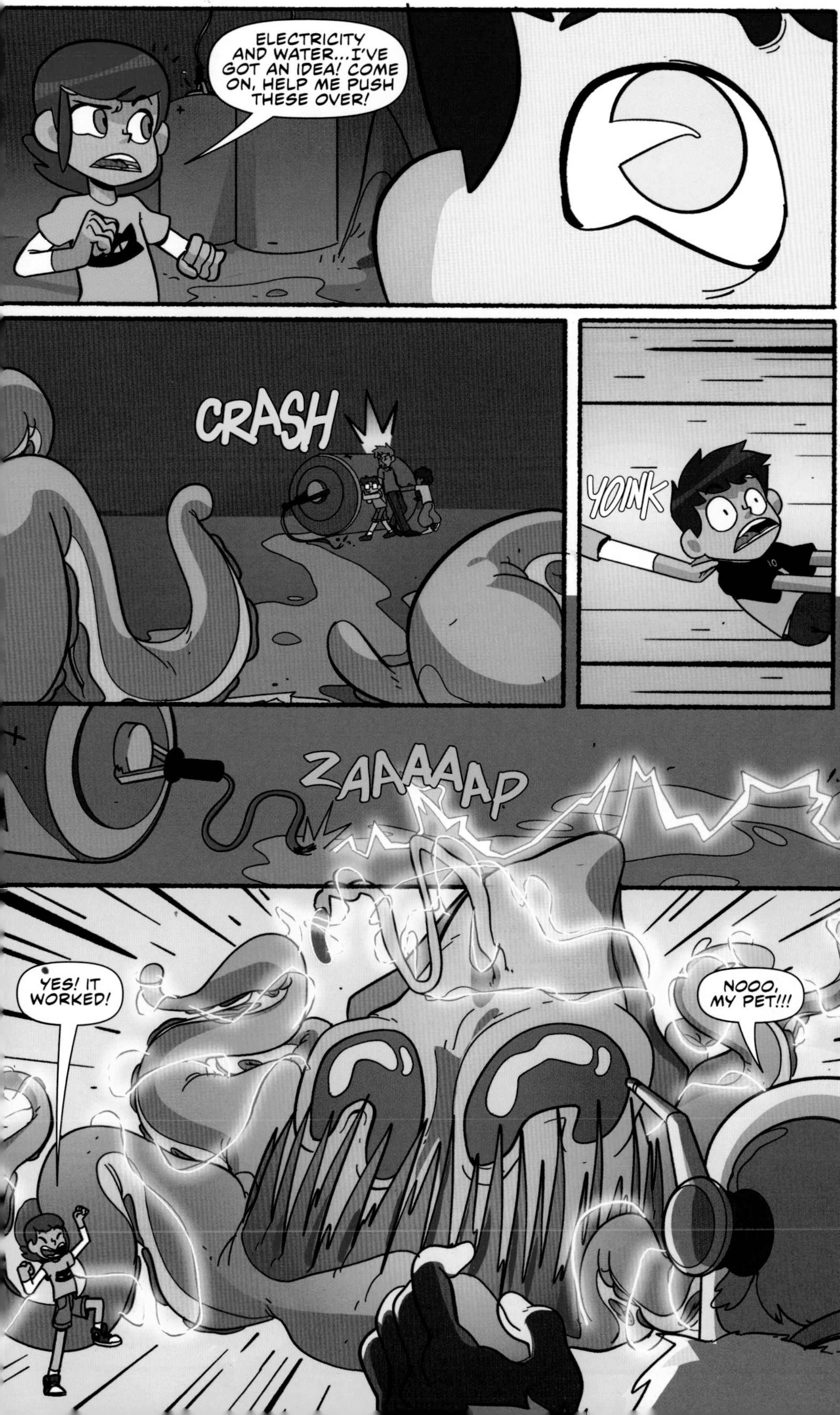
ELECTRICITY AND WATER...I'VE GOT AN IDEA! COME ON, HELP ME PUSH THESE OVER!
CRASH
YOINK
ZAAAAAP
YES! IT WORKED!
NOOO, MY PET!!!

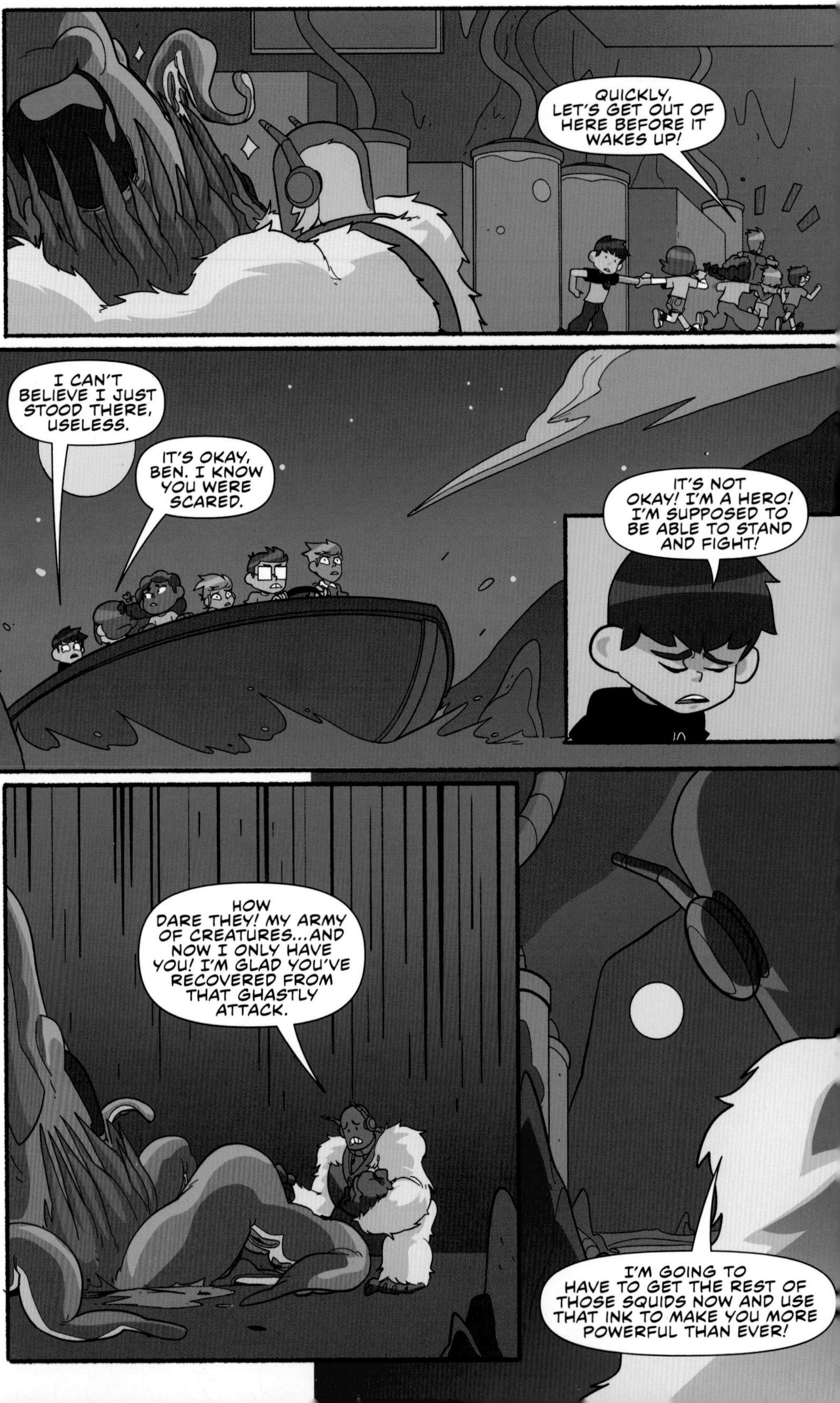
QUICKLY, LET'S GET OUT OF HERE BEFORE IT WAKES UP!
I CAN'T BELIEVE I JUST STOOD THERE, USELESS.
IT'S OKAY, BEN. I KNOW YOU WERE SCARED.
IT'S NOT OKAY! I'M A HERO! I'M SUPPOSED TO BE ABLE TO STAND AND FIGHT!
HOW DARE THEY! MY ARMY OF CREATURES...AND NOW I ONLY HAVE YOU! I'M GLAD YOU'VE RECOVERED FROM THAT GHASTLY ATTACK.
I'M GOING TO HAVE TO GET THE REST OF THOSE SQUIDS NOW AND USE THAT INK TO MAKE YOU MORE POWERFUL THAN EVER!

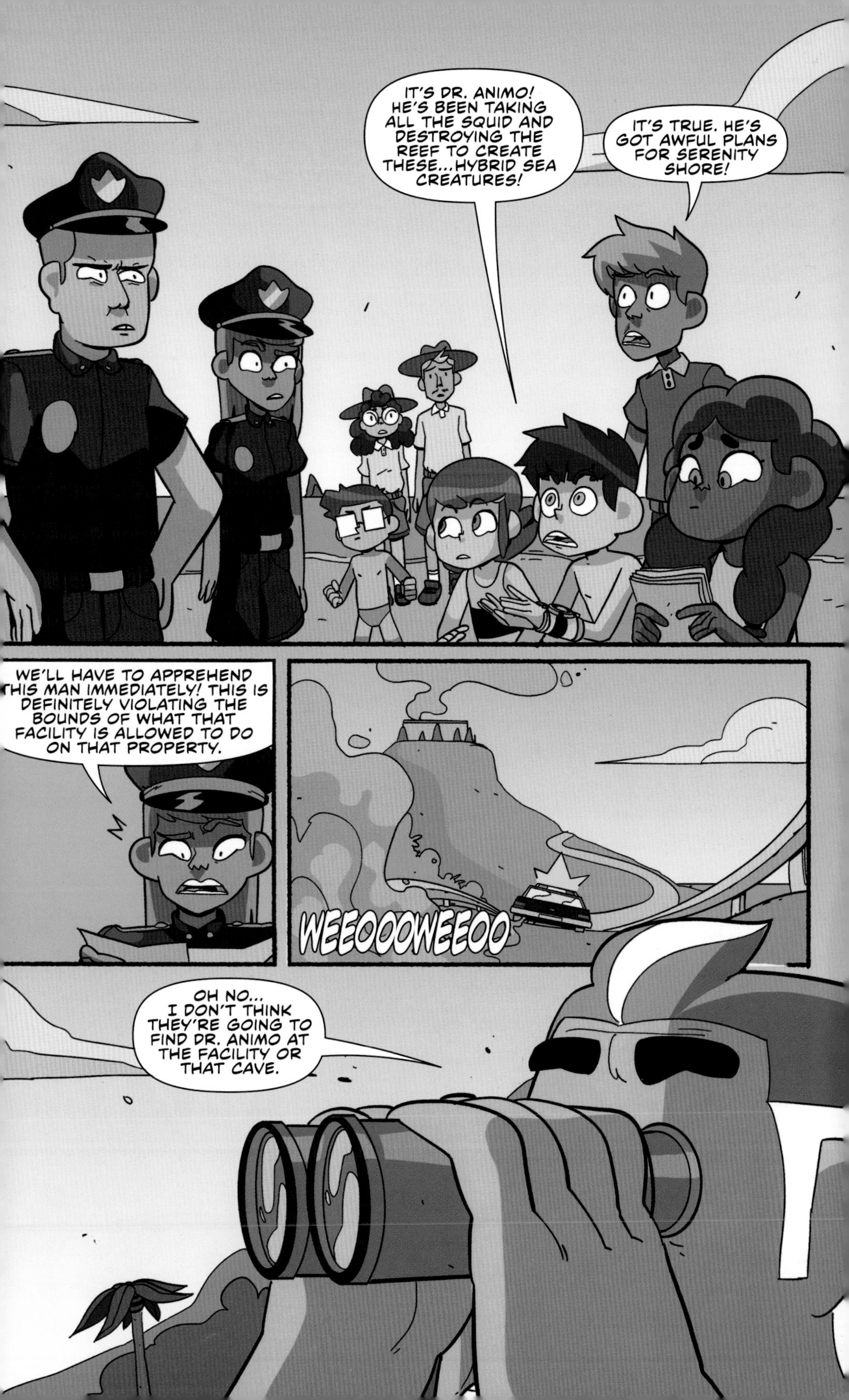
IT'S DR. ANIMO! HE'S BEEN TAKING ALL THE SQUID AND DESTROYING THE REEF TO CREATE THESE...HYBRID SEA CREATURES!
IT'S TRUE. HE'S GOT AWFUL PLANS FOR SERENITY SHORE!
WE'LL HAVE TO APPREHEND THIS MAN IMMEDIATELY! THIS IS DEFINITELY VIOLATING THE BOUNDS OF WHAT THAT FACILITY IS ALLOWED TO DO ON THAT PROPERTY.
WEEOOOWEEOO
OH NO... I DON'T THINK THEY'RE GOING TO FIND DR. ANIMO AT THE FACILITY OR THAT CAVE.

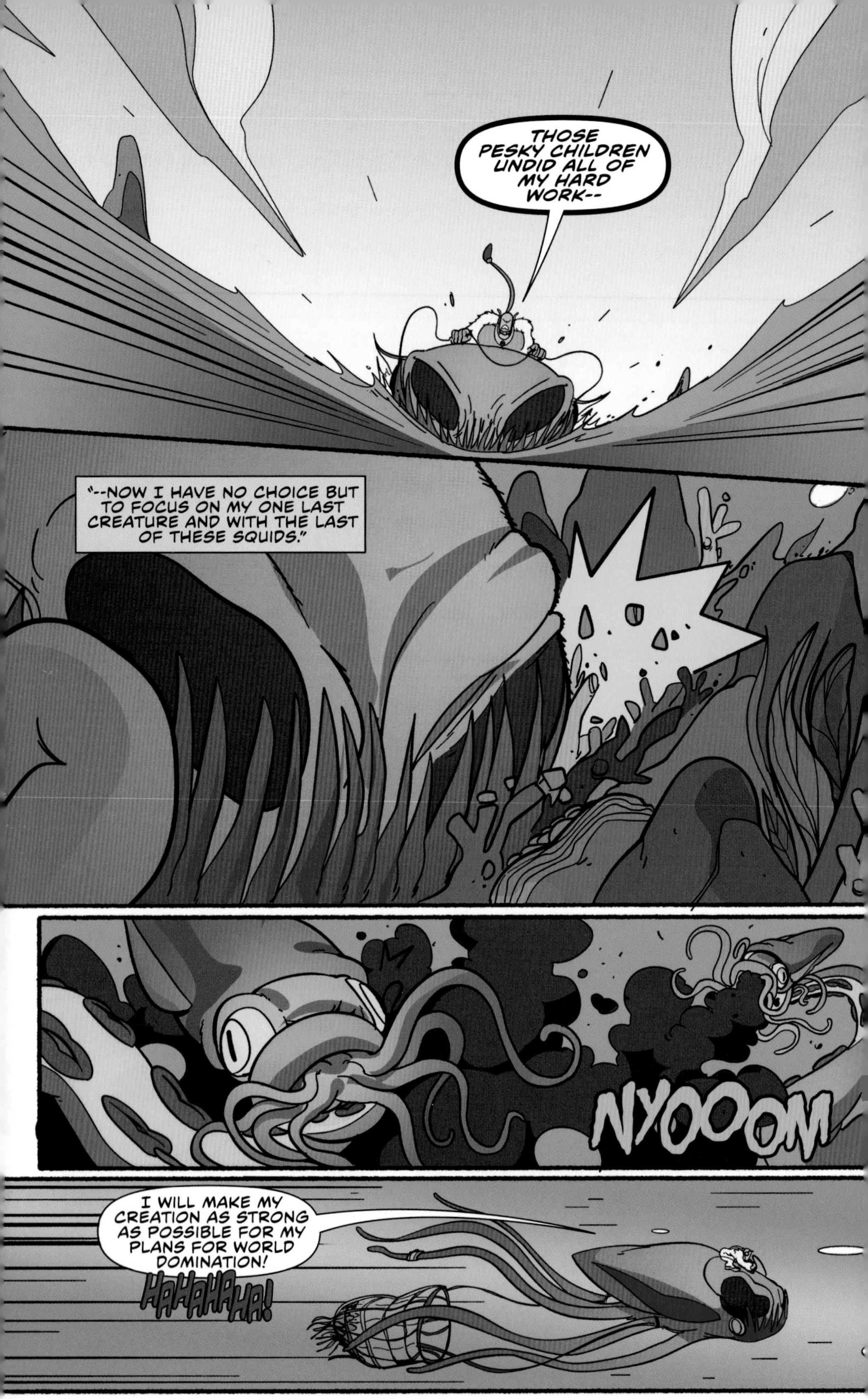
THOSE PESKY CHILDREN UNDID ALL OF MY HARD WORK--
"--NOW I HAVE NO CHOICE BUT TO FOCUS ON MY ONE LAST CREATURE AND WITH THE LAST OF THESE SQUIDS."
NYOOOM
I WILL MAKE MY CREATION AS STRONG AS POSSIBLE FOR MY PLANS FOR WORLD DOMINATION!
HAHAHAHAHA!

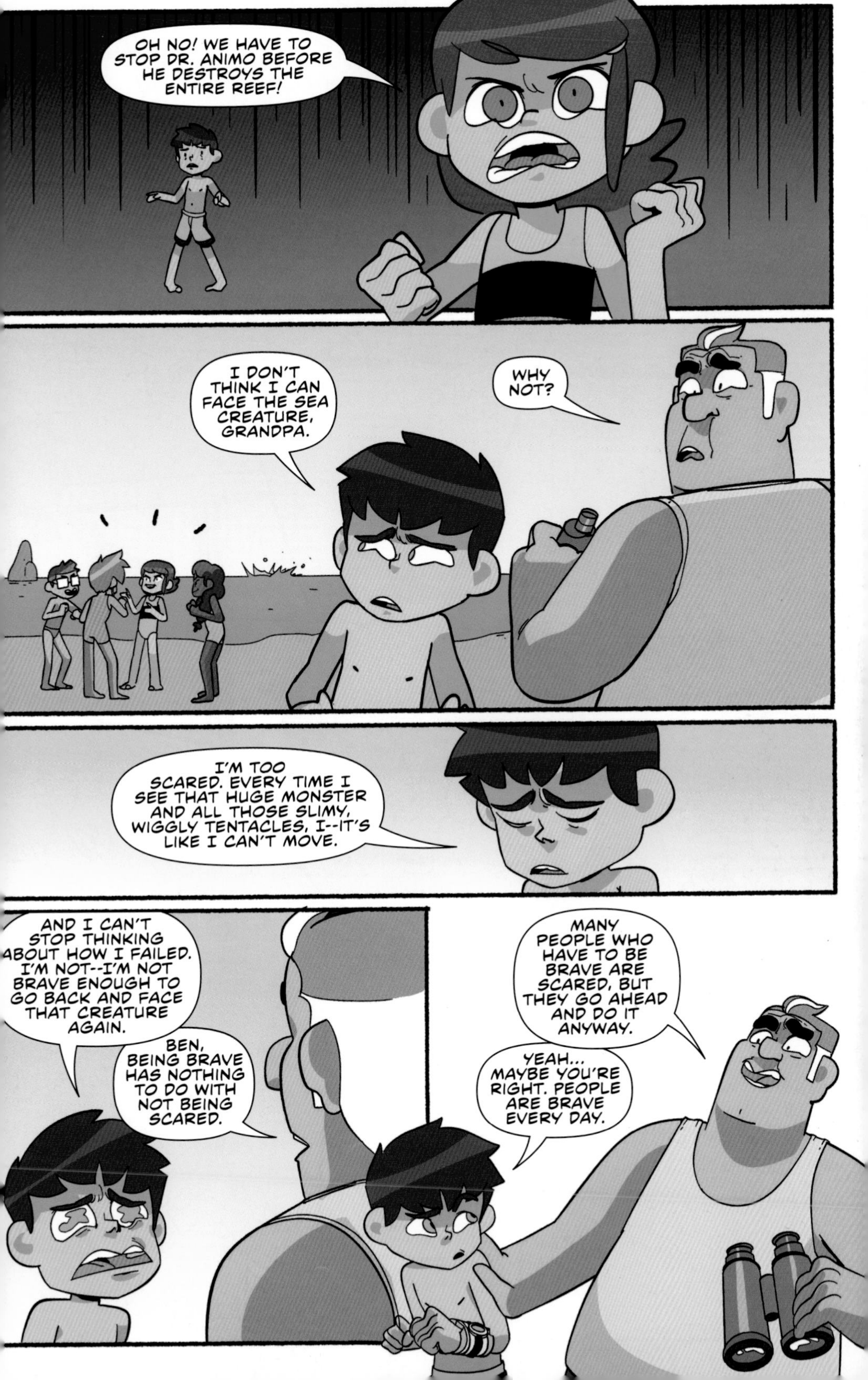
OH NO! WE HAVE TO STOP DR. ANIMO BEFORE HE DESTROYS THE ENTIRE REEF!
I DON'T THINK I CAN FACE THE SEA CREATURE, GRANDPA.
WHY NOT?
I'M TOO SCARED. EVERY TIME I SEE THAT HUGE MONSTER AND ALL THOSE SLIMY, WIGGLY TENTACLES, I--IT'S LIKE I CAN'T MOVE.
AND I CAN'T STOP THINKING ABOUT HOW I FAILED. I'M NOT--I'M NOT BRAVE ENOUGH TO GO BACK AND FACE THAT CREATURE AGAIN.
BEN, BEING BRAVE HAS NOTHING TO DO WITH NOT BEING SCARED.
MANY PEOPLE WHO HAVE TO BE BRAVE ARE SCARED, BUT THEY GO AHEAD AND DO IT ANYWAY.
YEAH... MAYBE YOU'RE RIGHT. PEOPLE ARE BRAVE EVERY DAY.

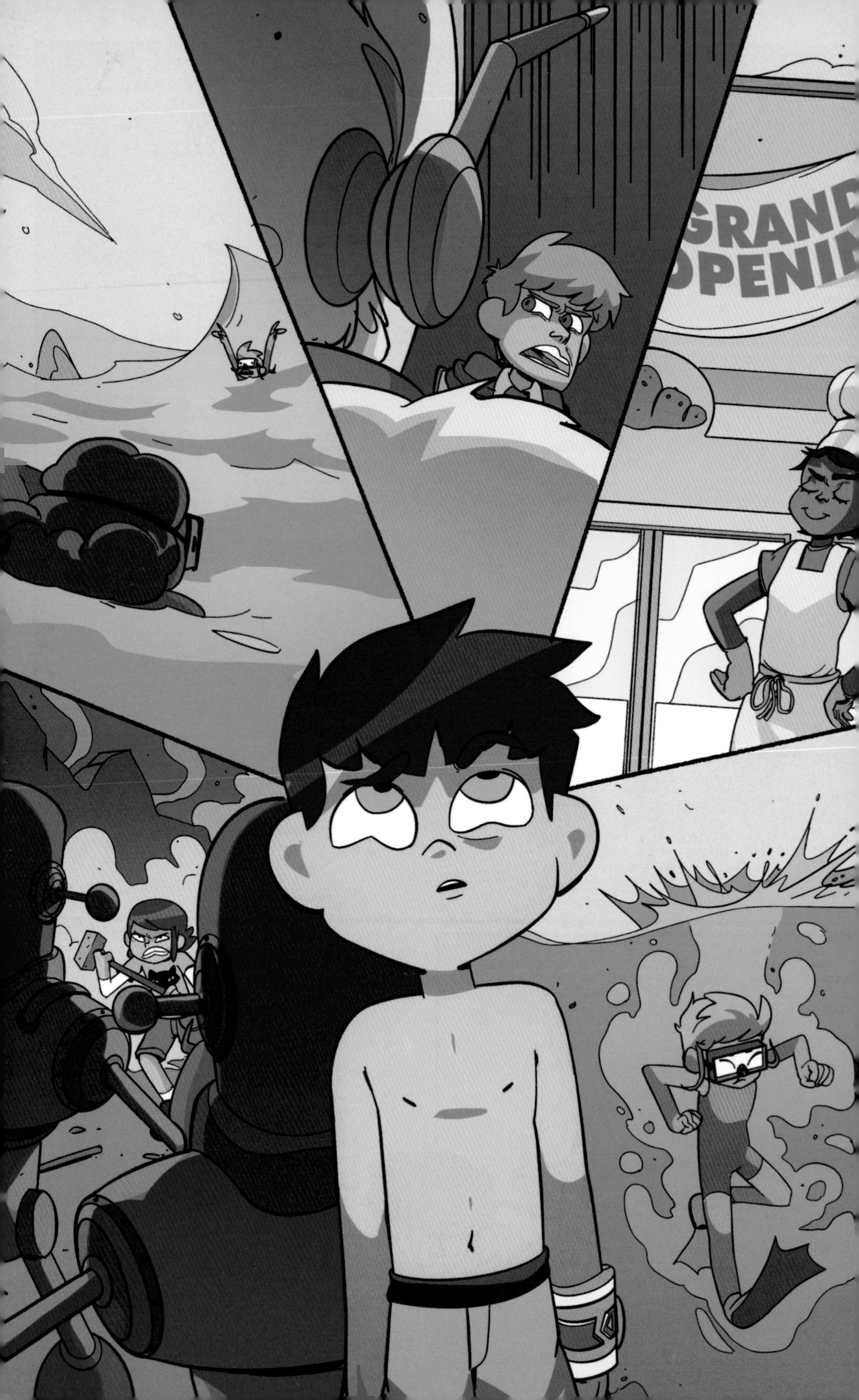
GRAND

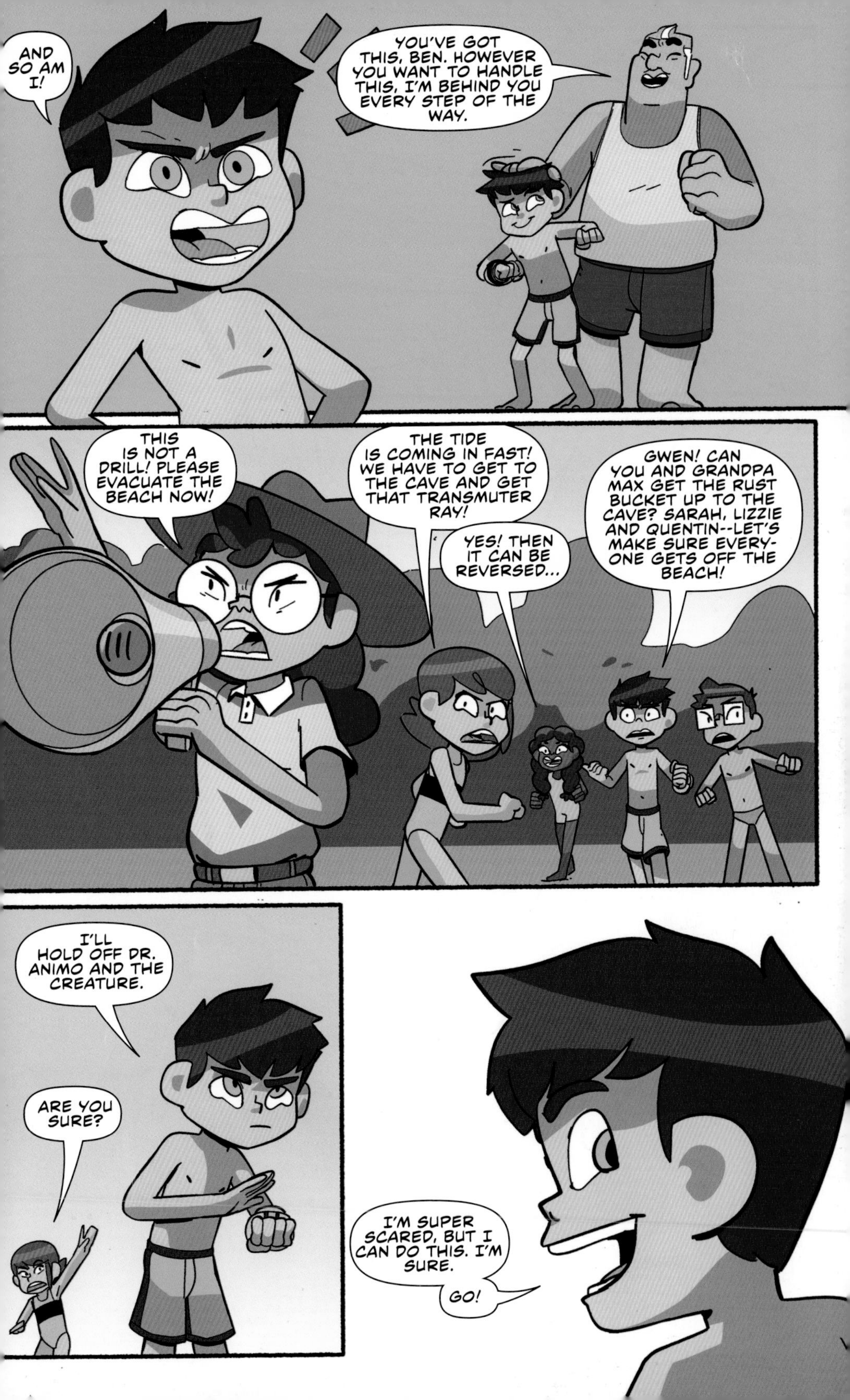
AND SO AM I!
YOU'VE GOT THIS, BEN. HOWEVER YOU WANT TO HANDLE THIS, I'M BEHIND YOU EVERY STEP OF THE WAY.
THIS IS NOT A DRILL! PLEASE EVACUATE THE BEACH NOW!
THE TIDE IS COMING IN FAST! WE HAVE TO GET TO THE CAVE AND GET THAT TRANSMUTER RAY!
YES! THEN IT CAN BE REVERSED...
GWEN! CAN YOU AND GRANDPA MAX GET THE RUST BUCKET UP TO THE CAVE? SARAH, LIZZIE AND QUENTIN--LET'S MAKE SURE EVERY-ONE GETS OFF THE BEACH!
I'LL HOLD OFF DR. ANIMO AND THE CREATURE.
ARE YOU SURE?
I'M SUPER SCARED, BUT I CAN DO THIS. I'M SURE.
GO!

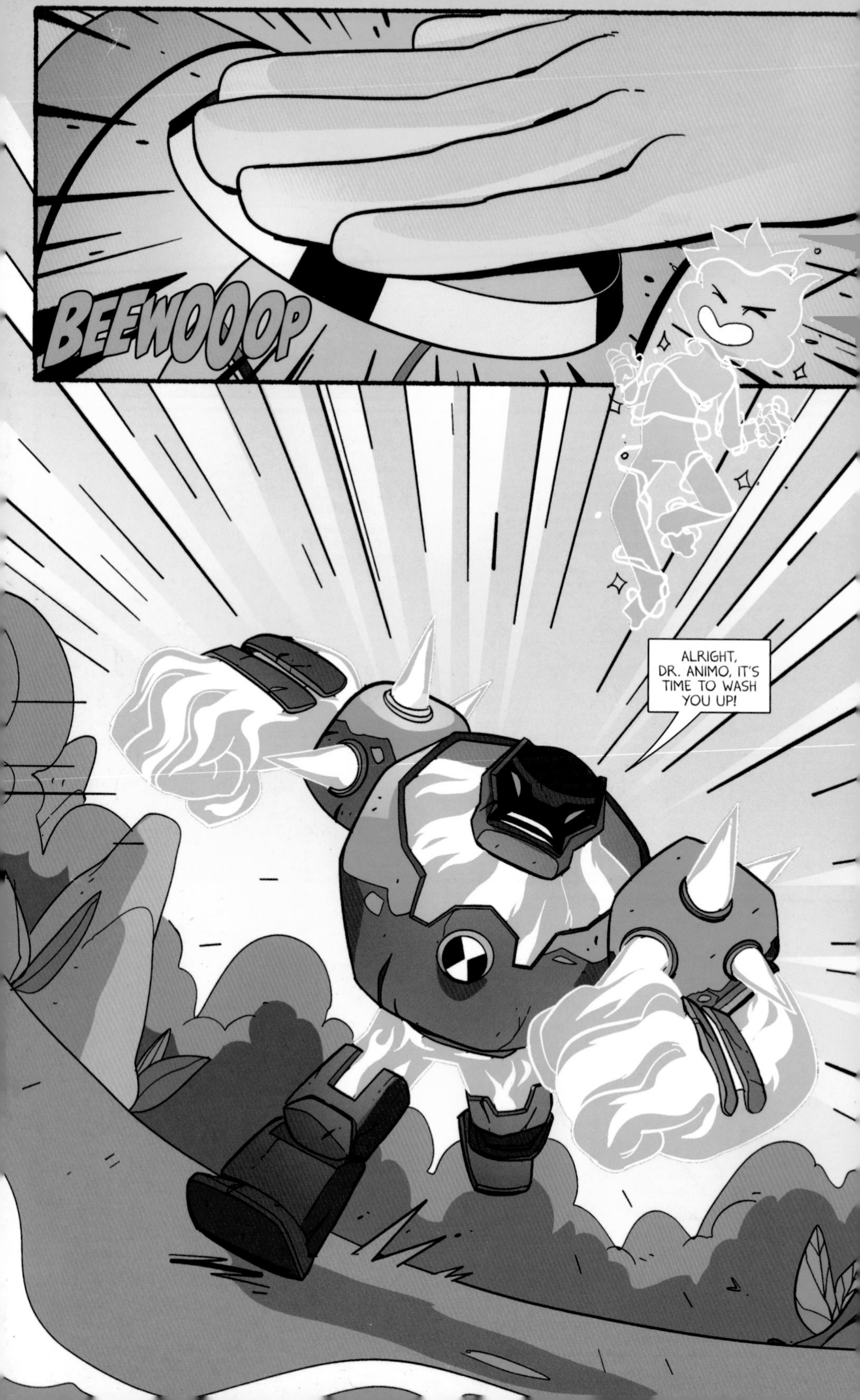
BEEWOOOP
ALRIGHT, DR. ANIMO, IT'S TIME TO WASH YOU UP!

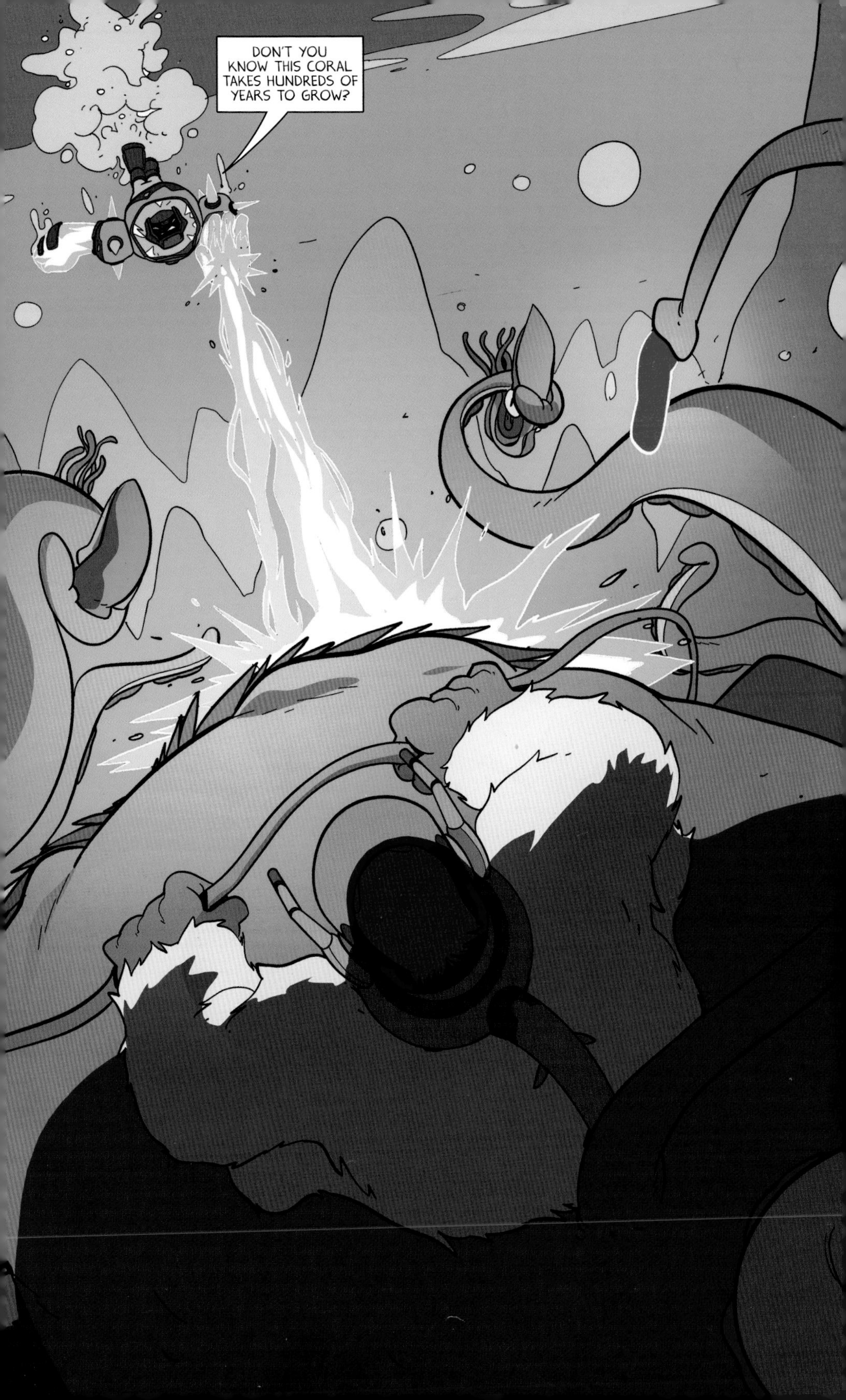
DON'T YOU KNOW THIS CORAL TAKES HUNDREDS OF YEARS TO GROW?

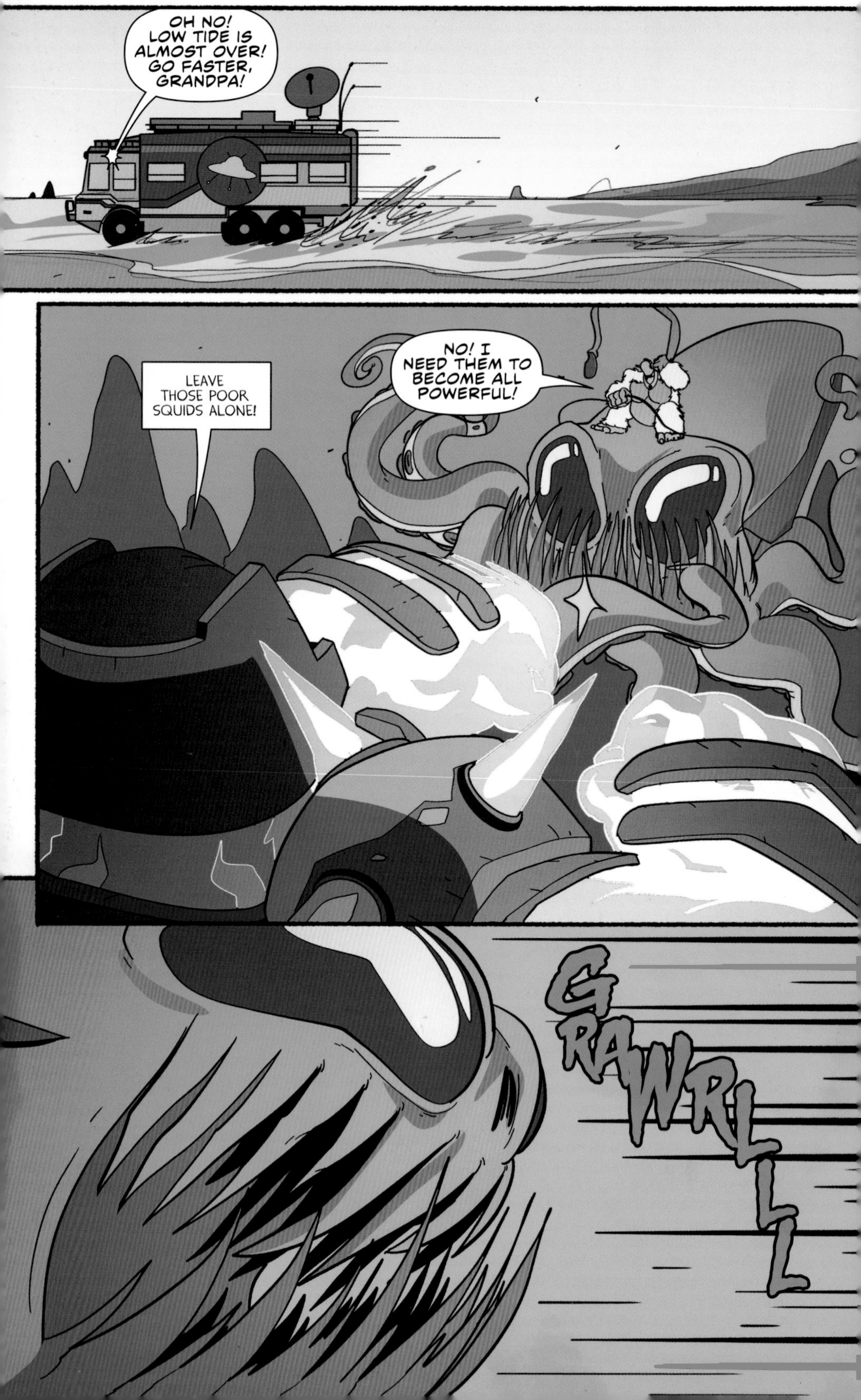
OH NO! LOW TIDE IS ALMOST OVER! GO FASTER, GRANDPA!
LEAVE THOSE POOR SQUIDS ALONE!
NO! I NEED THEM TO BECOME ALL POWERFUL!
GRAWRLLL

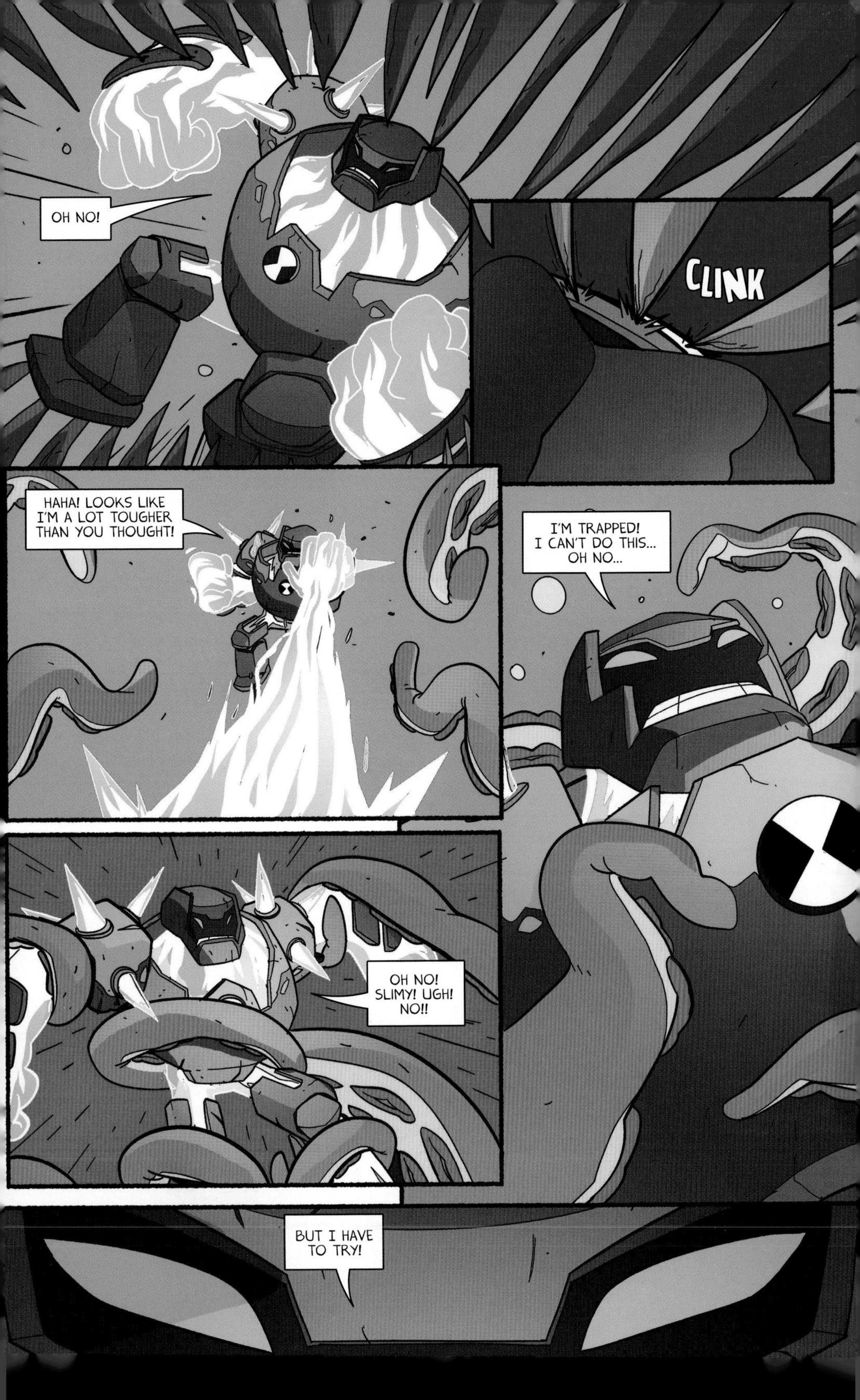
OH NO!
CLINK
HAHA! LOOKS LIKE I'M A LOT TOUGHER THAN YOU THOUGHT!
I'M TRAPPED! I CAN'T DO THIS... OH NO...
OH NO! SLIMY! UGH! NO!!
BUT I HAVE TO TRY!

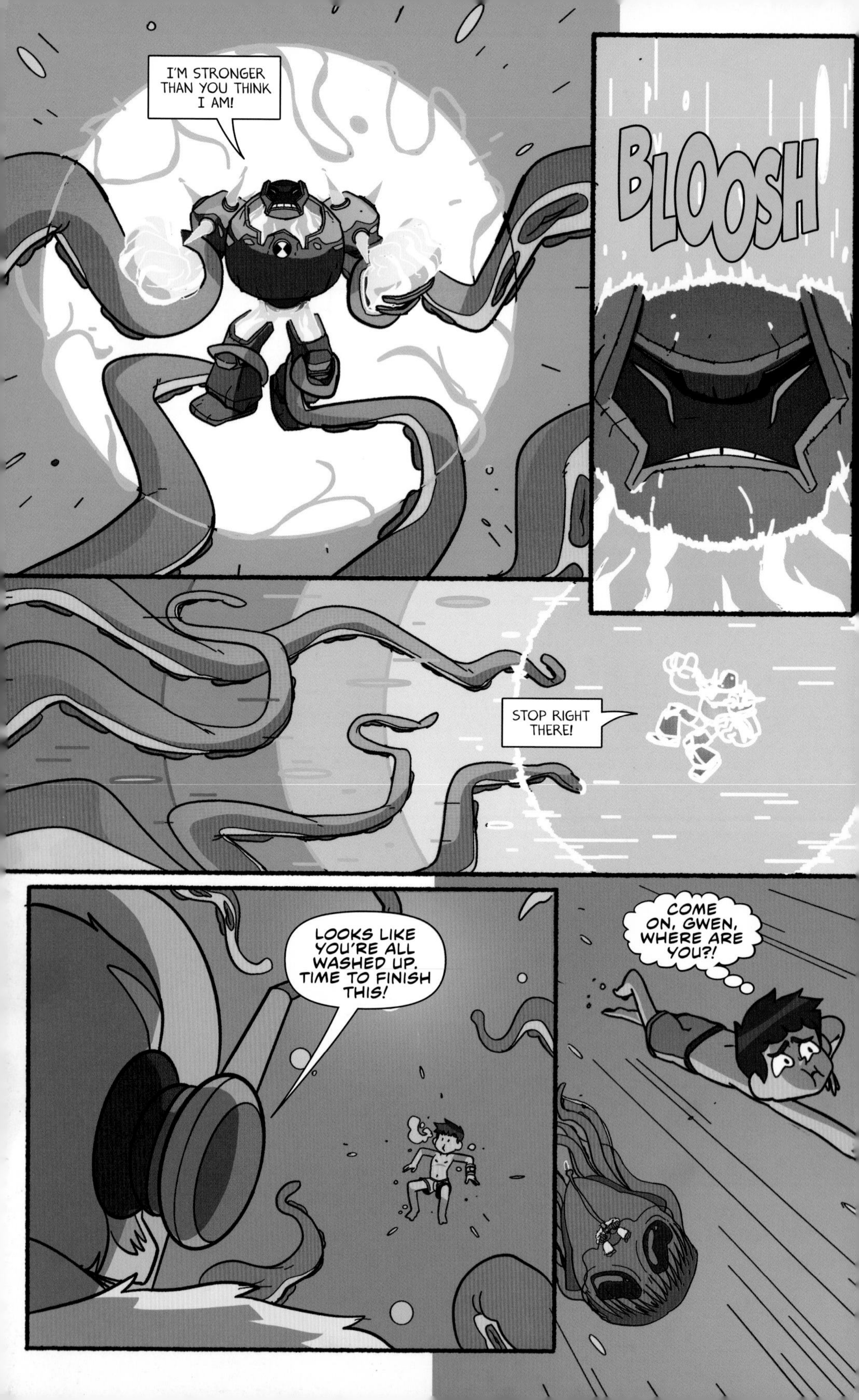
I'M STRONGER THAN YOU THINK I AM!
BLOOSH
STOP RIGHT THERE!
LOOKS LIKE YOU'RE ALL WASHED UP. TIME TO FINISH THIS!
COME ON, GWEN, WHERE ARE YOU?!

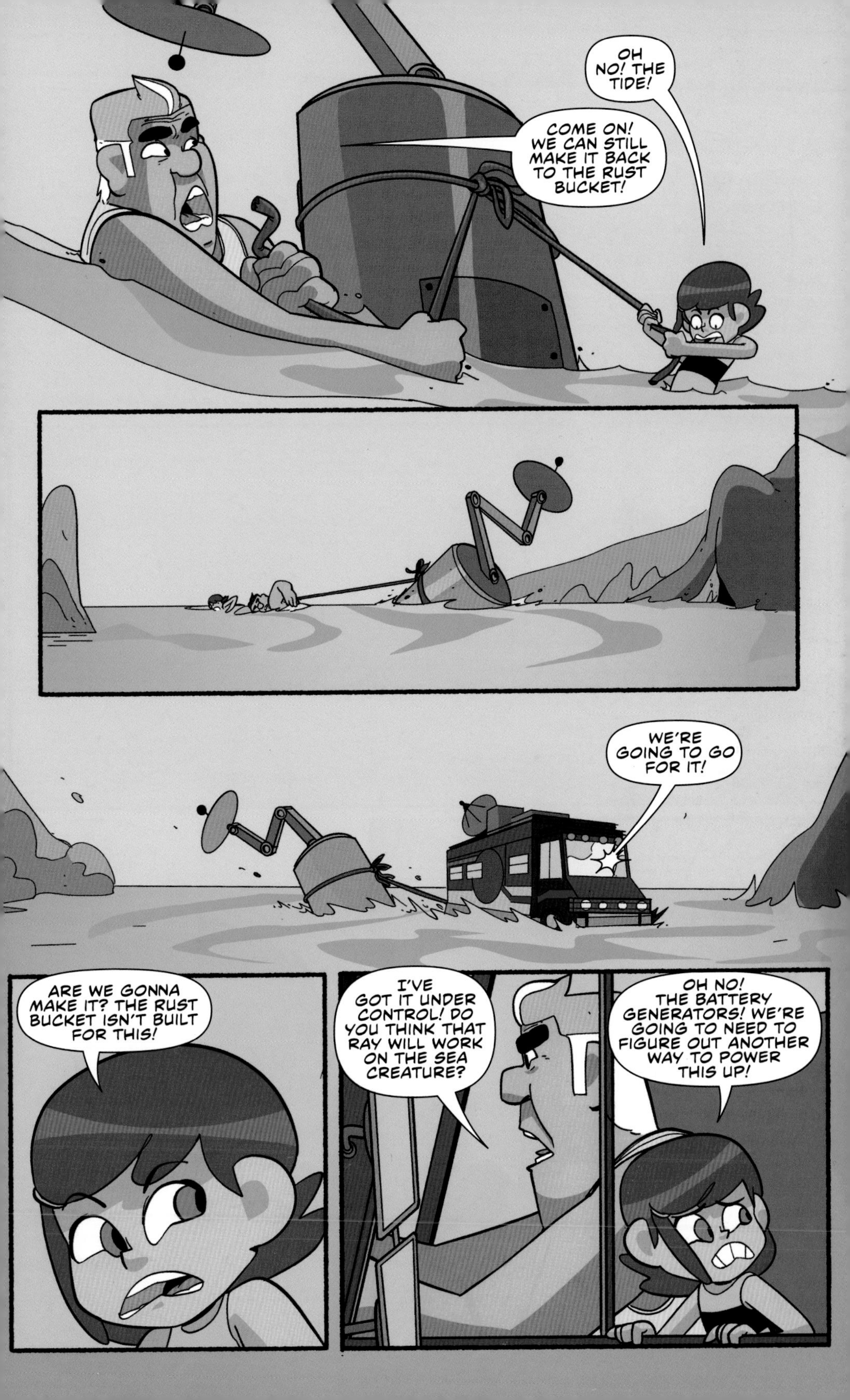
OH NO! THE TIDE!
COME ON! WE CAN STILL MAKE IT BACK TO THE RUST BUCKET!
WE'RE GOING TO GO FOR IT!
ARE WE GONNA MAKE IT? THE RUST BUCKET ISN'T BUILT FOR THIS!
I'VE GOT IT UNDER CONTROL! DO YOU THINK THAT RAY WILL WORK ON THE SEA CREATURE?
OH NO! THE BATTERY GENERATORS! WE'RE GOING TO NEED TO FIGURE OUT ANOTHER WAY TO POWER THIS UP!

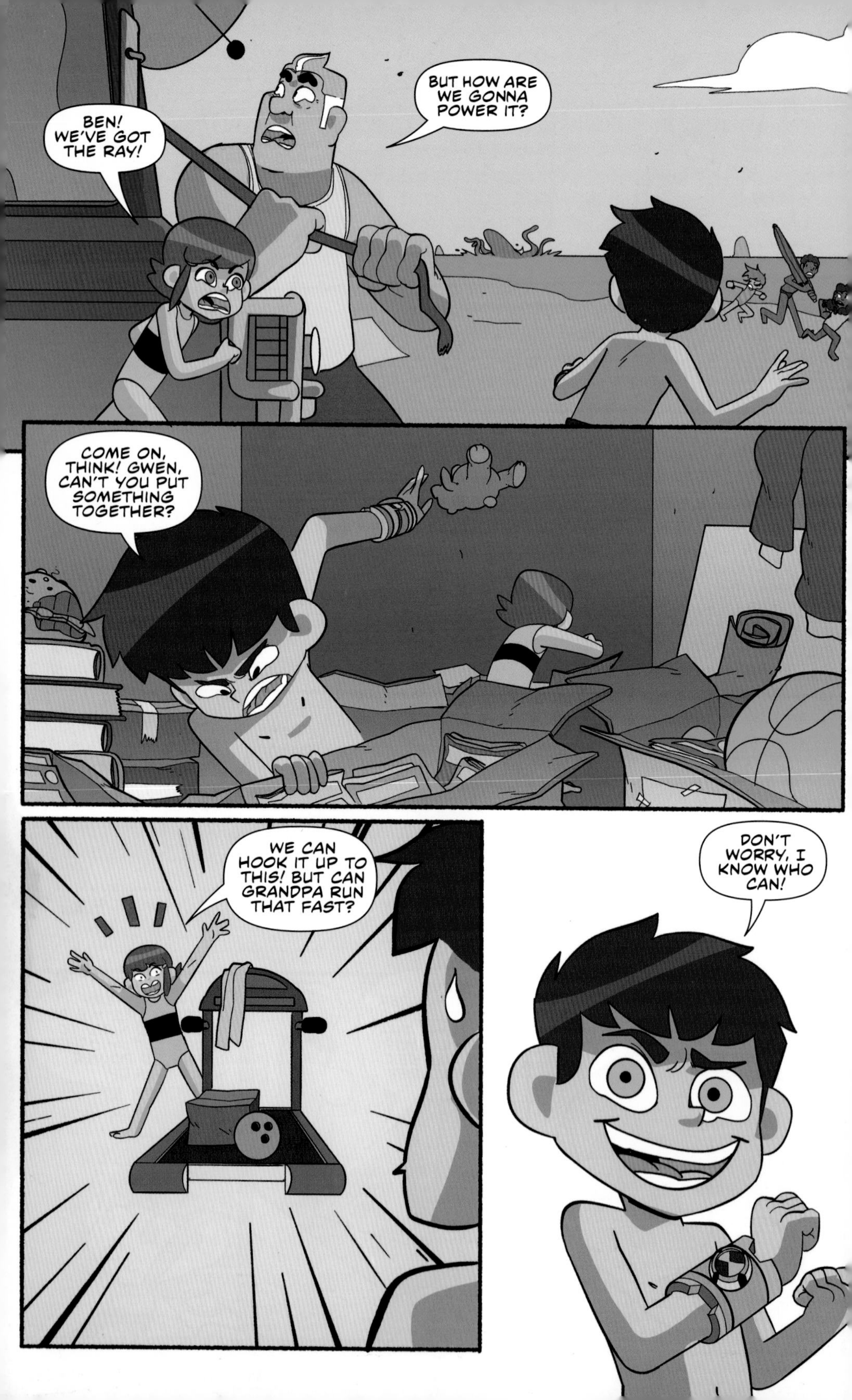
BEN! WE'VE GOT THE RAY!
BUT HOW ARE WE GONNA POWER IT?
COME ON, THINK! GWEN, CAN'T YOU PUT SOMETHING TOGETHER?
WE CAN HOOK IT UP TO THIS! BUT CAN GRANDPA RUN THAT FAST?
DON'T WORRY, I KNOW WHO CAN!

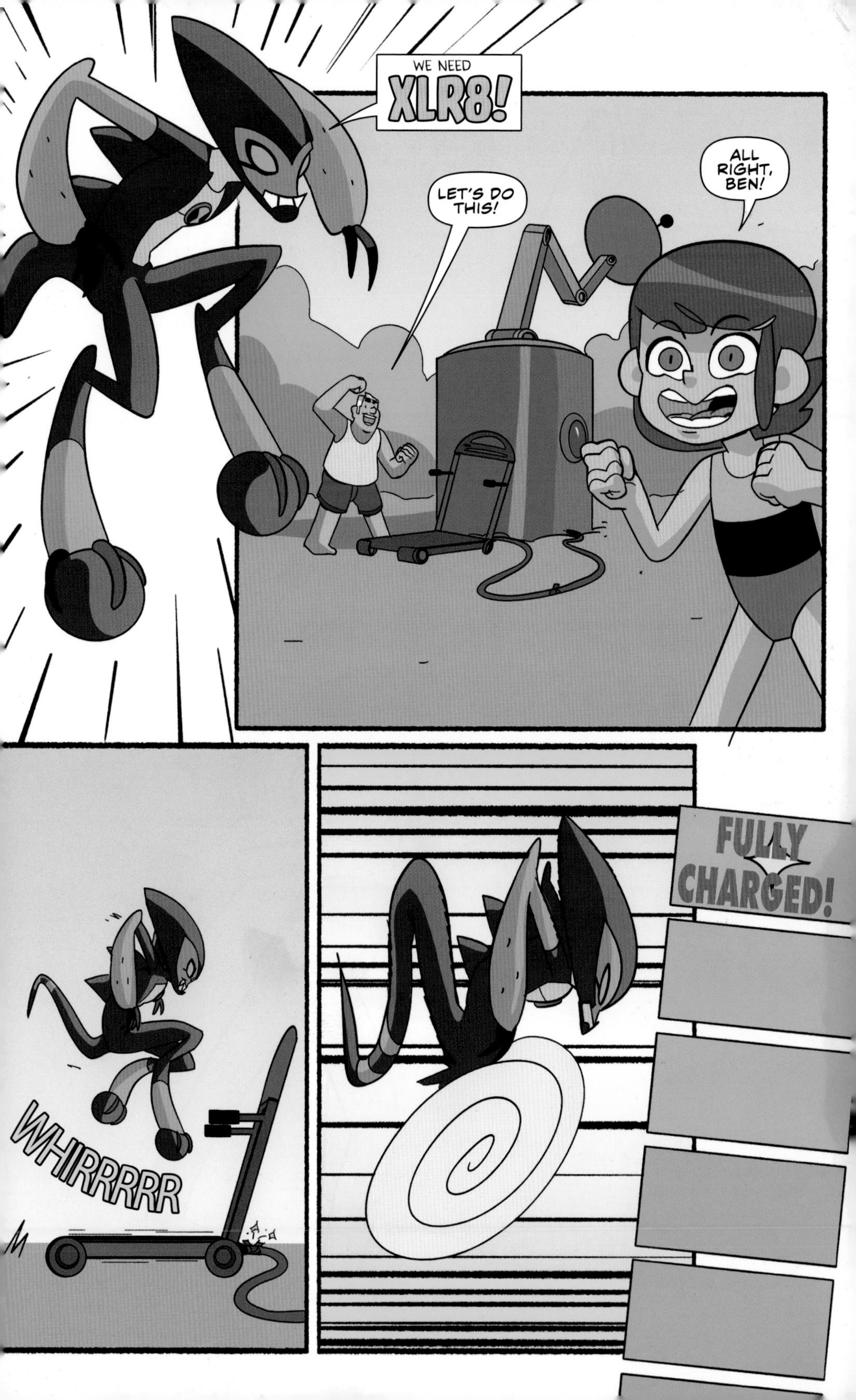
WE NEED
XLR8!
LET'S DO THIS!
ALL RIGHT, BEN!
WHIRRRRRR
FULLY CHARGED!

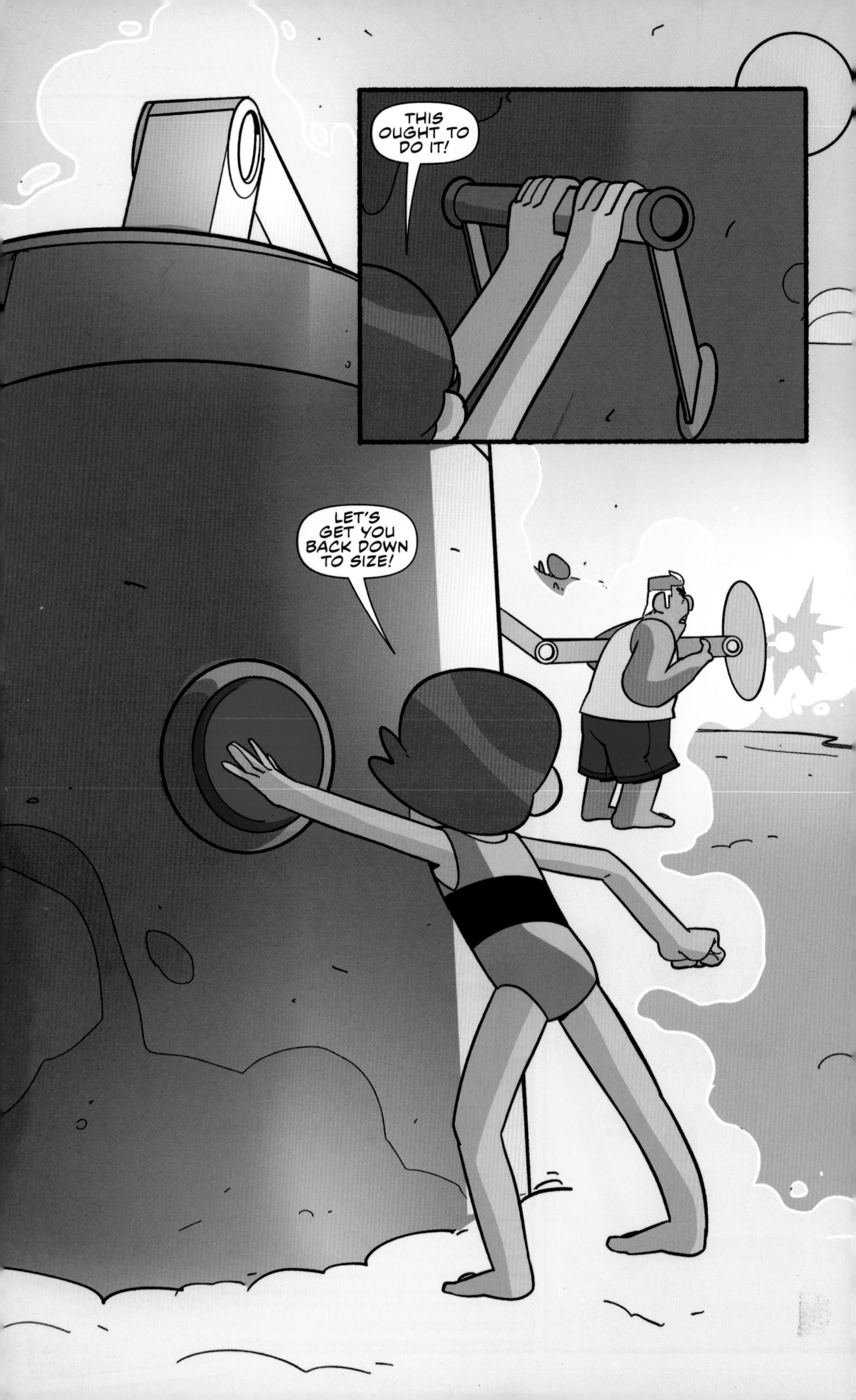
THIS OUGHT TO DO IT!
LET'S GET YOU BACK DOWN TO SIZE!

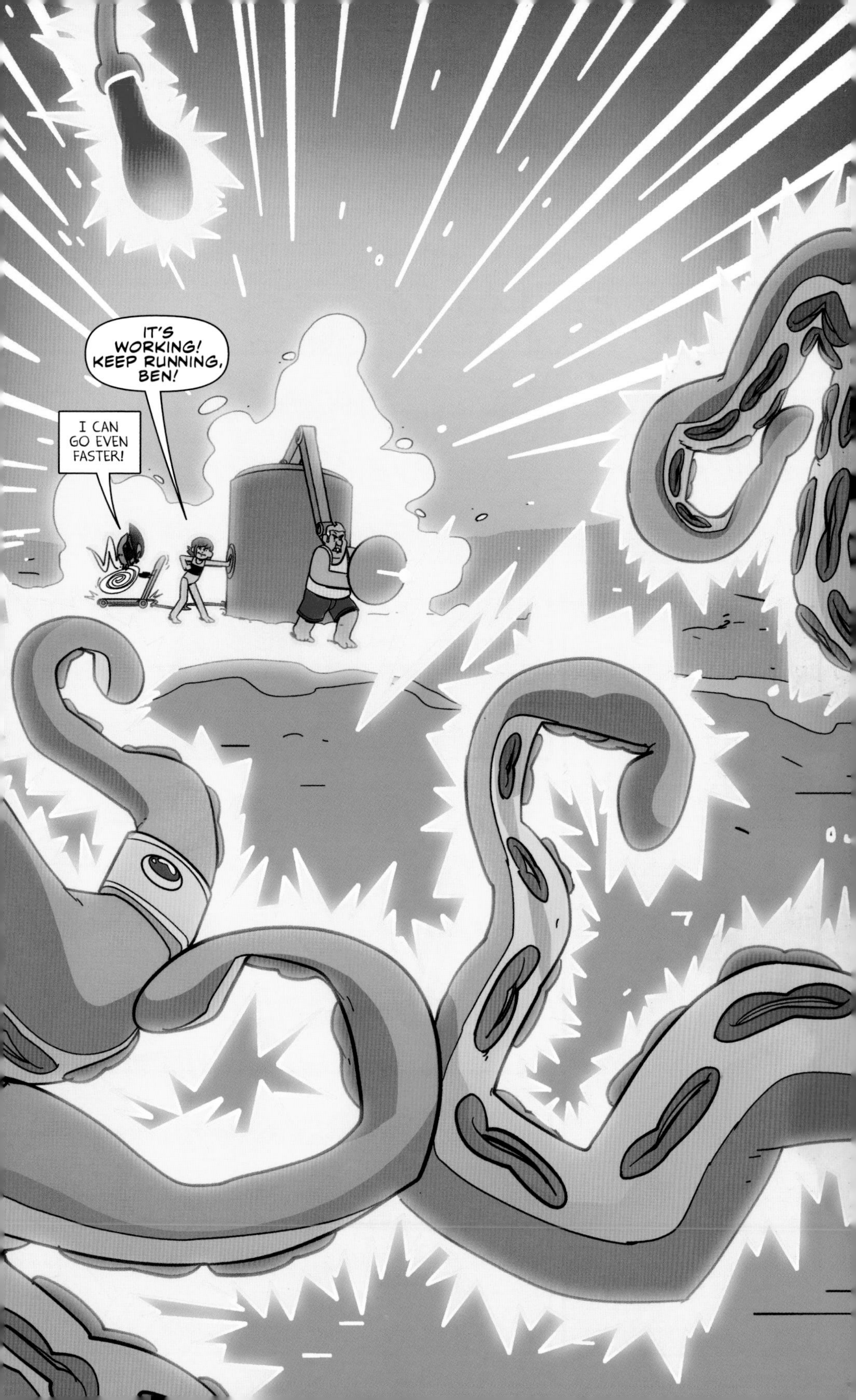
IT'S WORKING! KEEP RUNNING, BEN!
I CAN GO EVEN FASTER!

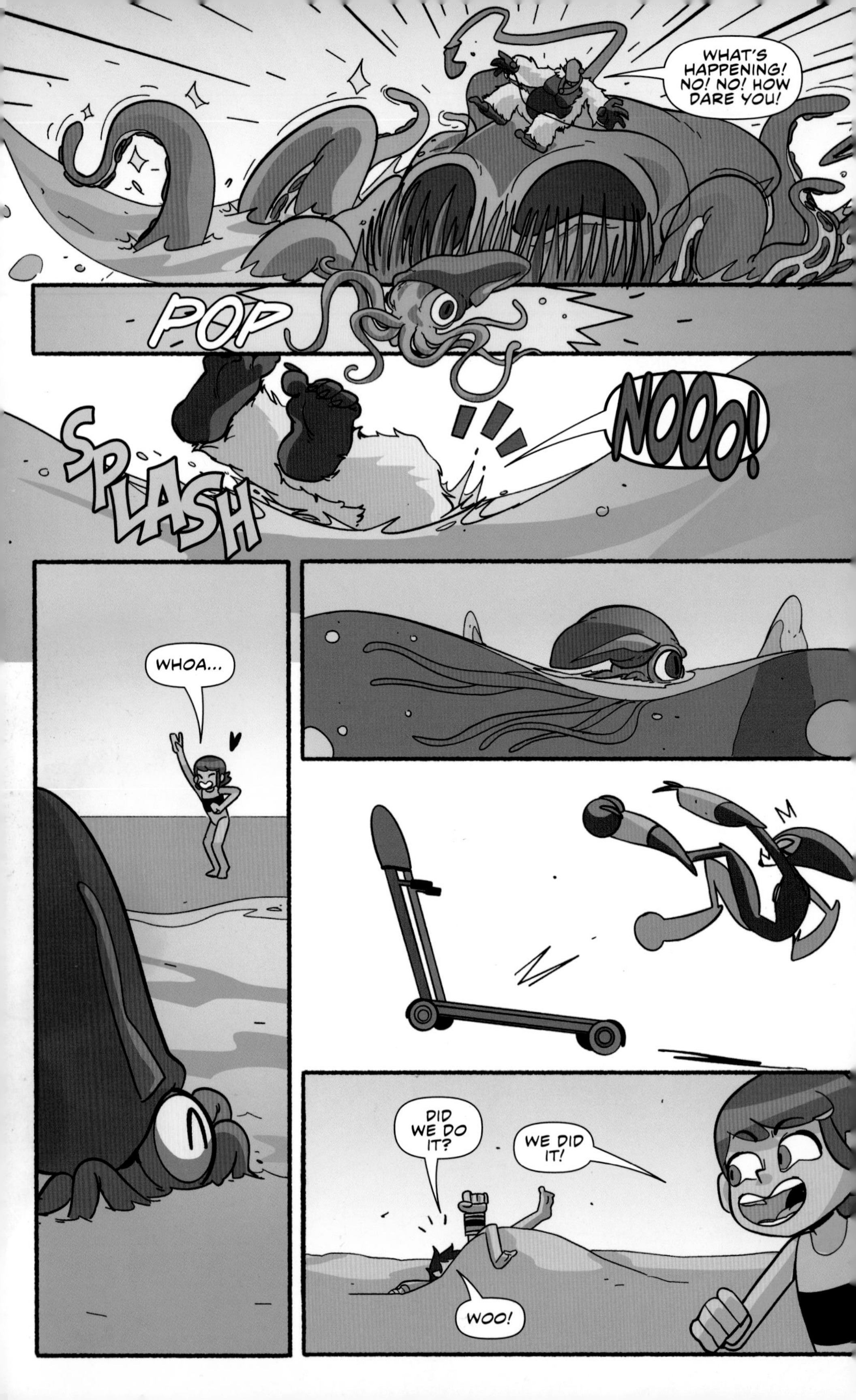
WHAT'S HAPPENING! NO! NO! HOW DARE YOU!
POP
SPLASH
NOOO!
WHOA...
DID WE DO IT?
WE DID IT!
WOO!

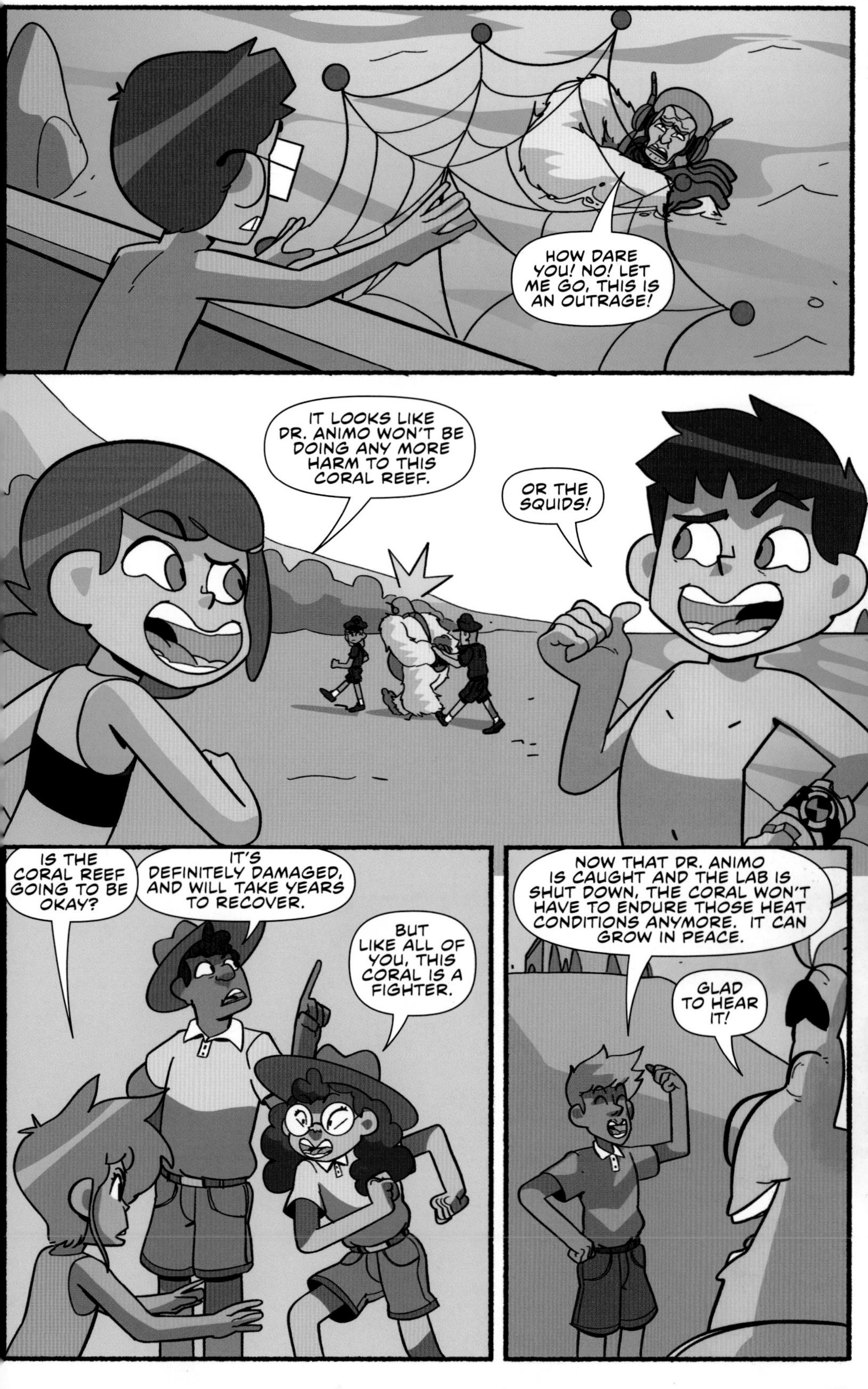
HOW DARE YOU! NO! LET ME GO, THIS IS AN OUTRAGE!
IT LOOKS LIKE DR. ANIMO WON'T BE DOING ANY MORE HARM TO THIS CORAL REEF.
OR THE SQUIDS!
IS THE CORAL REEF GOING TO BE OKAY?
IT'S DEFINITELY DAMAGED, AND WILL TAKE YEARS TO RECOVER.
BUT LIKE ALL OF YOU, THIS CORAL IS A FIGHTER.
NOW THAT DR. ANIMO IS CAUGHT AND THE LAB IS SHUT DOWN, THE CORAL WON'T HAVE TO ENDURE THOSE HEAT CONDITIONS ANYMORE. IT CAN GROW IN PEACE.
GLAD TO HEAR IT!

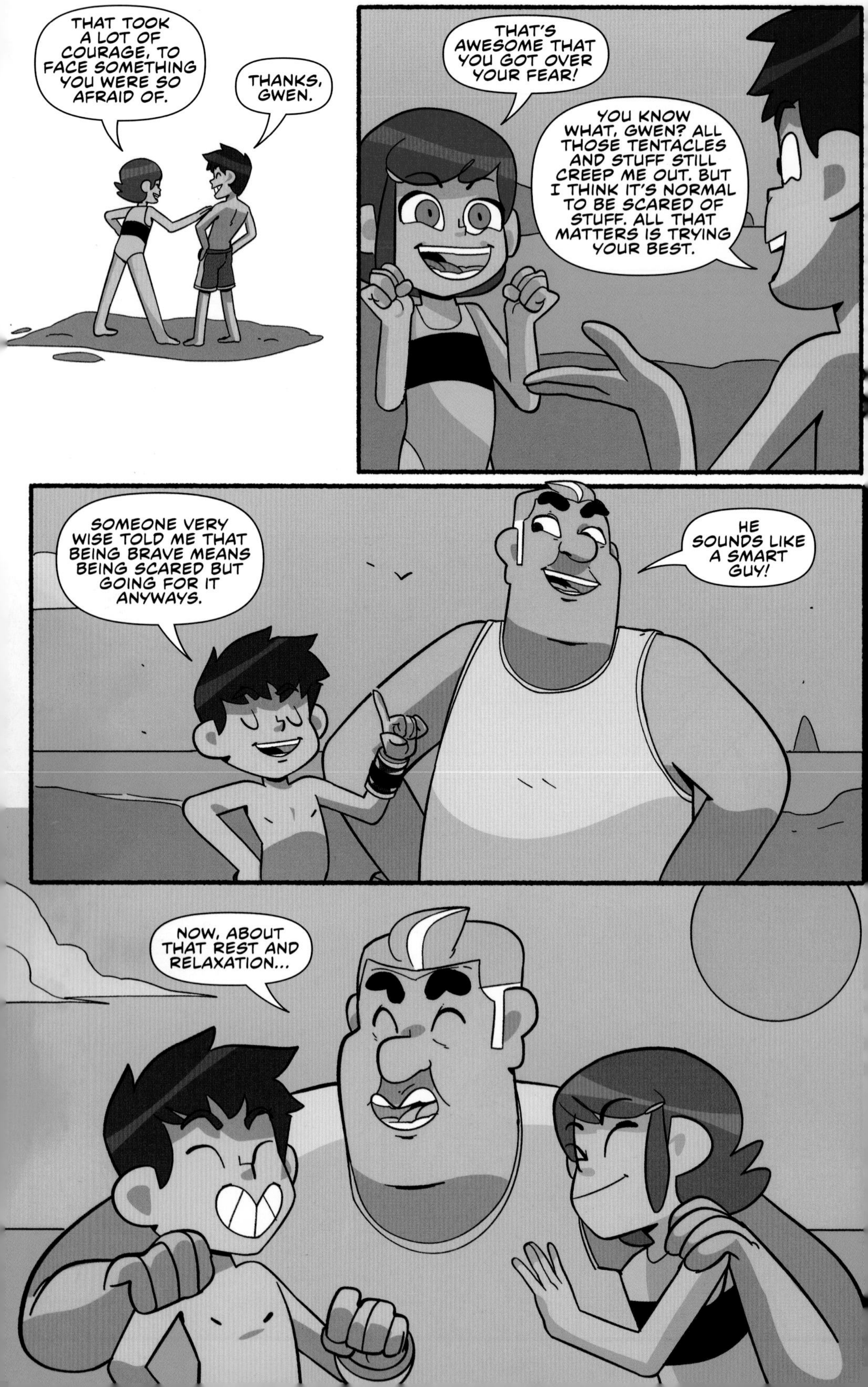
THAT TOOK A LOT OF COURAGE, TO FACE SOMETHING YOU WERE SO AFRAID OF.
THANKS, GWEN.
THAT'S AWESOME THAT YOU GOT OVER YOUR FEAR!
YOU KNOW WHAT, GWEN? ALL THOSE TENTACLES AND STUFF STILL CREEP ME OUT. BUT I THINK IT'S NORMAL TO BE SCARED OF STUFF. ALL THAT MATTERS IS TRYING YOUR BEST.
SOMEONE VERY WISE TOLD ME THAT BEING BRAVE MEANS BEING SCARED BUT GOING FOR IT ANYWAYS.
HE SOUNDS LIKE A SMART GUY!
NOW, ABOUT THAT REST AND RELAXATION...

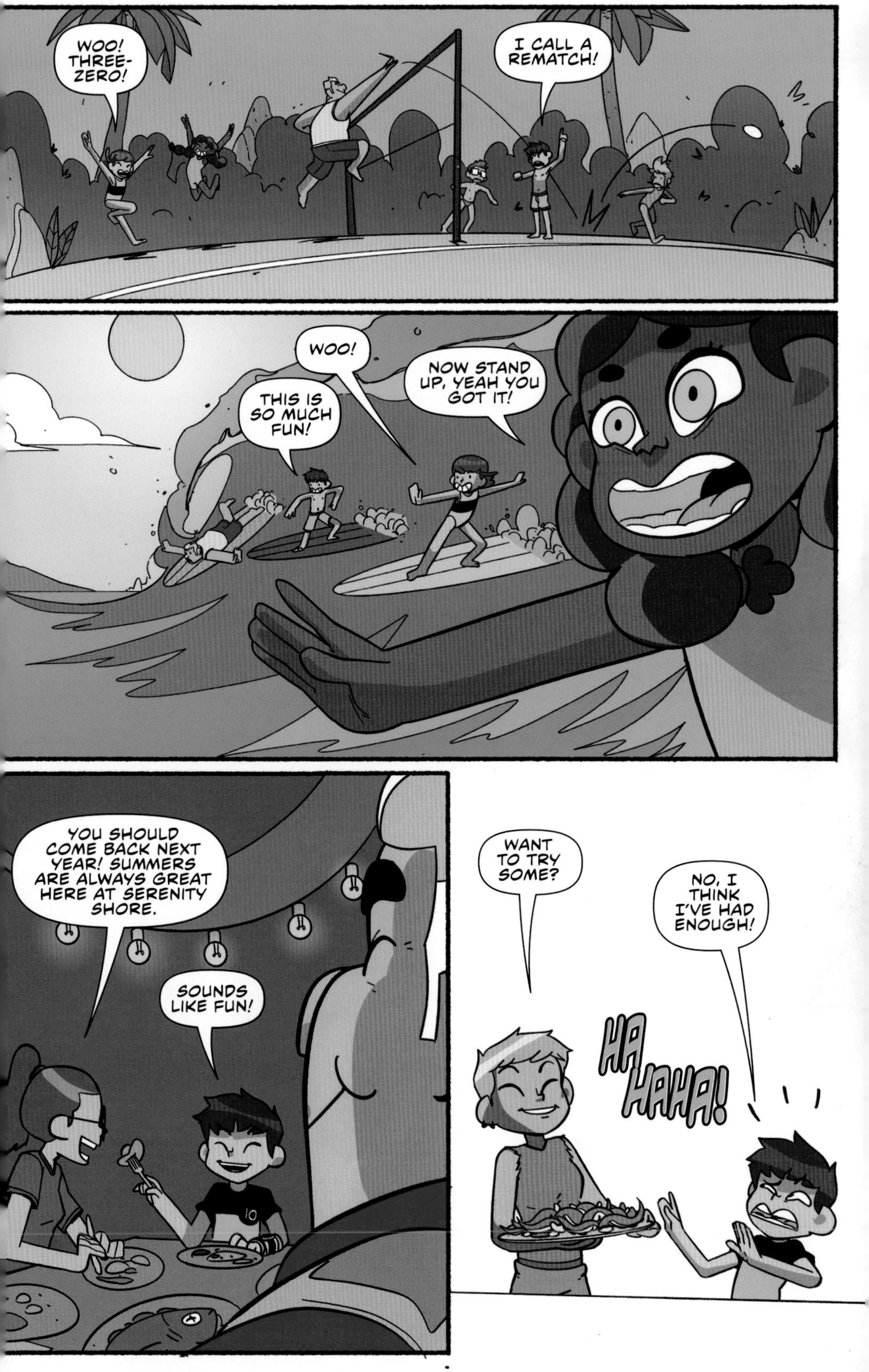
WOO! THREE-ZERO!
I CALL A REMATCH!
WOO!
THIS IS SO MUCH FUN!
NOW STAND UP, YEAH YOU GOT IT!
YOU SHOULD COME BACK NEXT YEAR! SUMMERS ARE ALWAYS GREAT HERE AT SERENITY SHORE.
SOUNDS LIKE FUN!
WANT TO TRY SOME?
NO, I THINK I'VE HAD ENOUGH!
HA HAHA!

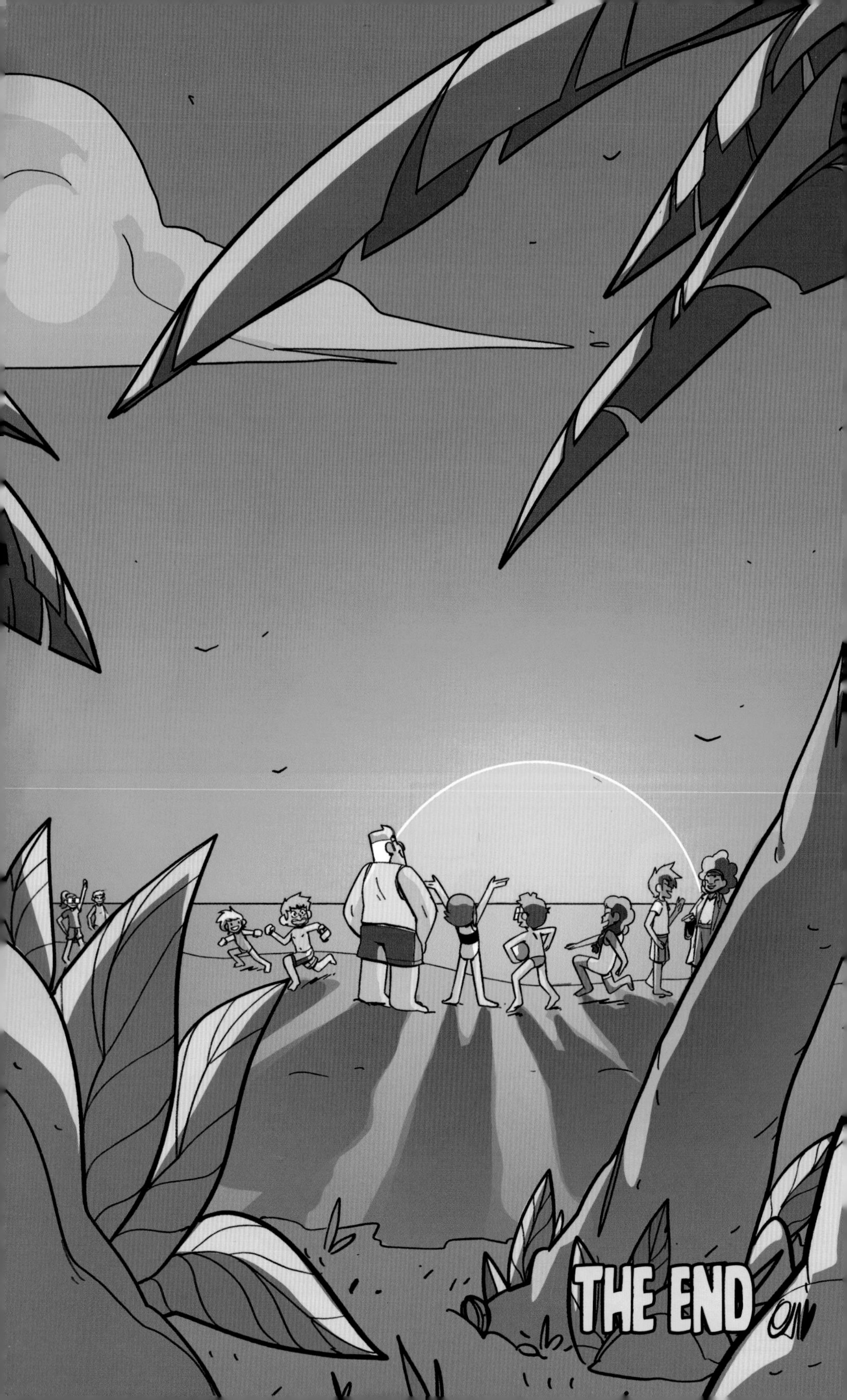
THE END

THE ADVENTURES IN THE RUSTBUCKET CONTINUE!

CATCH UP ON ALL OF BEN, GWEN, AND GRANDPA MAX'S ADVENTURES IN...

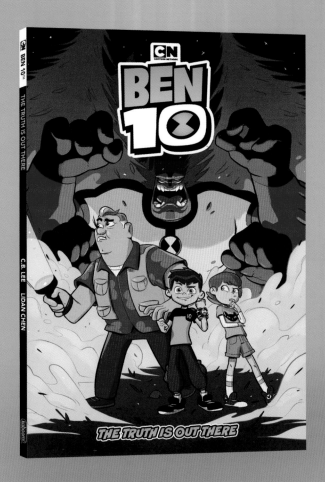

"FOR SCIENCE!"

AVAILABLE NOW

CN
BEN 10™
FOR SCIENCE!
C.B. LEE
MATTIA DI MEO
kaboom!
BEN 10
FOR SCIENCE!

WRITTEN BY

C.B. LEE

ILLUSTRATED BY

MATTIA DI MEO

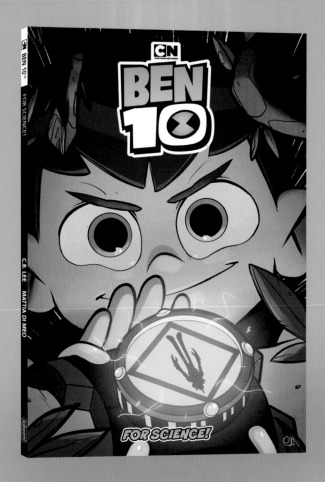

"MECHA MADNESS"

AVAILABLE NOW

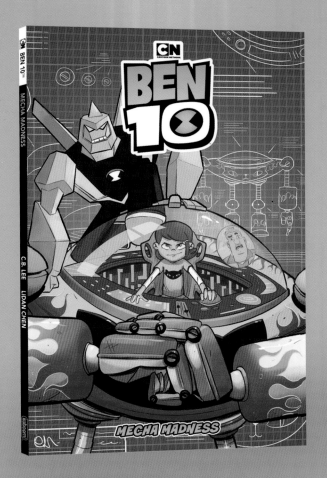

WRITTEN BY
C.B. LEE

ILLUSTRATED BY
LIDAN CHEN

"THE MANCHESTER MYSTERY"

AVAILABLE NOW

WRITTEN BY
C.B. LEE

ILLUSTRATED BY
FRANCESCA PERRONE

DISCOVER
EXPLOSIVE NEW WORLDS

AVAILABLE AT YOUR LOCAL
COMICS SHOP AND BOOKSTORE
To find a comics shop in your area, visit www.comicshoplocator.com
WWW.**BOOM-STUDIOS**.COM